S0-AUZ-484

NIGHT

OF THE

FALLING STARS

By Terry and Wayne Baltz

NIGHT

OF THE

FALLING STARS

Terry and Wayne Baltz

Cover Design & Illustration by Gary Raham

To Allison
Terry Baltz
Wayne Baltz

A Threshold Book

PRAIRIE DIVIDE PRODUCTIONS

Fort Collins, Colorado

This is a work of fiction. It does, however, incorporate historical settings, characters, legends, and events. A selected bibliography is included at the end of the story for further reading.

Copyright © 1995 by Terry and Wayne Baltz.
All rights reserved.
Published by   Prairie Divide Productions
                    305 W. Magnolia, Suite 116
                    Fort Collins, CO 80521

Cover design and illustration © 1995 by Gary Raham.

Library of Congress Catalogue Card Number: 95-70986

Printed in the U.S.A.

ISBN 1-884610-51-X

For our parents

NIGHT

OF THE

FALLING STARS

Prologue

Once I had a friend.

A most unusual friend.

Part of the past, part of the present, she helped me create my future.

And then she was gone.

But for a time, fleeting as a falling star, our lives touched.

1

I sat up, gasping for breath, cold and shaking. Somewhere, someone was pounding on a door.

"Lisa? Are you all right?"

My mother's voice.

"I'm okay, Sandy," I called.

Am I, I wondered? I don't even know where I am. The room is wrong. This isn't my room.

"Lisa, let me in," Sandy said, her voice as calm and in control as always.

Still shaking, I swung my legs over the side of the bed. Cool, smooth tile on the soles of my feet forced me to remember: I was at the Hot Springs Lodge.

I opened the door. Bright light swept in from the hall, and Sandy with it. Her face was in shadow, and her slim form and blond hair tied in a ribbon made her look like a teenager. People mistook us for sisters. Often. Same brown eyes, same honey-blond hair. So similar in appearance, but so different in every other way.

"Did I scream again?" I asked. Sandy nodded. "I'm sorry."

Apologizing. Again. I hated myself for it.

She turned on the lamp and closed the door. Taking my hand, she eased me back to the bed and sat next to me.

There was no place else to sit. More like a prison cell than a hotel room, the tiny cubicle contained a bed, a chest of drawers, a night table and lamp, and hangers on hooks. No private bath. Not even a closet.

"Lisa, I'm sure the nightmares will stop soon. You'll feel a lot better after we move into the new house."

"I don't think so," I said.

"While we're here maybe you could learn to swim or something." I refused to look at her. She wasn't making any headway with me and I wanted her to know it. "Well, anyway, we won't be staying at the Lodge much longer," she said.

"Good," I snapped. "I'm ready to leave now. Let's just pack up and go back home."

Home. Our eleventh floor apartment in St. Louis. Security entry, computerized heating and cooling. My bedroom with its own bath. My own balcony, from which I could watch — as if invisible — what went on in the city far below. How I longed for all that again.

And my father.

Sandy sighed. "Honey, that's the past. It's over. You've got to see that. To accept it."

I let Sandy's words roll past. In my mind's eye I could still see my father, sitting in his high-backed rocker, cradling the lopsided coffee mug I'd made for him in crafts class, warming his ever-cold fingers, surrounded by the floor-to-ceiling book shelves that lined the walls of his study.

"We can't go back," Sandy said, as if listening in on my thoughts.

2

"I'd feel better there," I said softly, trying to get through.

"I know you think that, Lisa —"

"I know what I feel." My voice was hard this time. I felt Sandy stiffen in response.

"I've got a job in Indian Springs, Lisa. We've got a new house. You'll have a chance to make friends." She was into The Speech now. I'd heard it all before. "You can feel good *here*," Sandy said. "If you want to."

"No, I can't," I said. And I don't want to try, I thought. "What new house, anyway? That broken down monstrosity you pointed out from the car when we got here? We'll be lucky if it has running water!"

Sandy stood up. She glared at me. "We've got a new life ahead of us."

"*You've* got a new life, Sandy. I just want to go back to St. Louis. I want my old life."

"I can't do anything about that. We couldn't go on living where we were, the way we were, on the little bit of money your father left."

Go ahead, I wanted to shout. Blame him. Because he cared more about ideas than money. Because he didn't plan on dying so young.

"I needed a job. I'm lucky I got one," she said, flinging the words at me like needles as she headed for the door.

"Well why couldn't you have gotten your big fancy job back home instead of in a crummy mountain town in Colorado?" I shouted at her retreating figure. The featureless hallway beyond her reminded me that there were people we didn't know behind every wall and door.

3

Sandy was silent. I began to wonder if I had pushed her over the line. It was something I couldn't know. In all my fifteen years it had never happened. I had never heard Sandy yell. Raise her voice, even. Or cry. Sandy believed in controlling her emotions. And she was good at it.

Finally, she spoke, her back still turned to me. "I didn't get a big fancy job," she said in measured tones to the empty hall. "And St. Louis is not our home anymore." When she turned there were red blotches on her neck and face and the little muscles at the back of her jaw pulsed rhythmically. "*This* is," she continued quietly. "I got a job *here*. You'll just have to get used to it, Lisa. We're here now."

Yeah. I'm here. But just until I get out of high school, I promised myself. Not a minute longer.

For a few moments we stared each other down. Then she moved soundlessly to the bed, took my face in her hands and kissed the top of my head. As if I'm a child, I thought. I was glad when she left, closing the door so gently, so quietly, behind her.

My face burned. Her control infuriated me. She hadn't even cried when Dad died. She'd always wanted to live in the west, the Rocky Mountains. It was Dad and I who kept her back. Now she had her way. I punched the pillow and planned my life. After high school, a big university in a big city. I didn't care where. Just not here.

The room was stifling. Its ceiling and walls closed in on me. And the only window, small and high off the floor, didn't seem to help. I climbed onto the night table to reach it. Pressing my forehead against the screen, I willed

4

the cool night air inside, and listened to the steady *whoosh* of vehicles from the highway.

All those cars. All those people. Going places.

I rolled my head on the screen and looked up into the night sky. A streak of light ripped the darkness. Almost immediately there was another, slashing the black sky white for a few seconds, then fading away. I watched and waited. Maybe a minute went by. I was losing interest when another trail of light ended in a startling flash of green.

Shooting stars. This must be the meteor shower I'd heard about on the radio. A big one that comes every August. Funny, I never noticed meteor showers back home. In fact, I could only remember seeing a few shooting stars in my whole life. Maybe all the city lights drowned them out. Maybe I never looked.

I don't know what it was — Sandy, the heat, the cars, maybe the stars — but I wanted out of that room. Now.

I threw a robe over my pajamas and padded out the door in my slippers, glad to see that the castle-size corridor was empty. People came out of their rooms all night long to use the bathrooms down the hall. I cringed at the thought that a complete stranger could emerge from one of the rooms at any moment and see me scurrying by in my night clothes.

Our rooms were on the second floor. A large balcony, overhanging the pool, opened off our hallway. The door stood open. I hurried out, relieved to find it empty. Cool mountain air, softened by the steamy warmth of the huge hot springs pool below, caressed my face. A slight smell of rotten eggs rose from the sulfurous water.

The balcony was L-shaped. Around the corner I found a spot where the lights of the building didn't intrude on the darkness. I leaned against a wooden railing and looked down into the pool. In the mist rising off the hot water I saw images of my father: his smile, his warm eyes, his long slender fingers. Suddenly, standing and awake, I was plunged back into my nightmare.

. . . crawling through a dark tunnel, pulling myself along by my fingers, scraping my knees on the rocky ground. The chill of damp earth creeps through my body. I don't want to go any further, but something pushes me on. Some part of me that has to know.

I inch forward, almost falling into a gaping hole. I peer down. Into a grave. His grave. His flesh rotted away. A skeleton laughing at me . . .

I pressed my fists into my eyes and shook my head hard, trying to break the nightmare's hold. I looked up, counted shooting stars, concentrating on each one as if it were the only thing in the world. But it didn't help. My father's death mask was in the night sky, too. I strained to think of him as a spirit, freed of body and grave. I turned back to the pool and stared into the water. I chanted, "Spirit. Spirit. Spirit. Spirit."

The water below, so calm a moment earlier, began to swirl round and round, like a small whirlpool. Something was down there. Under the water. I held my breath. Not a body. Please, not a dead body.

I clasped the railing and closed my eyes. Get yourself together, I told myself. It's the middle of the night. The pool has been closed and the gates locked since ten. I forced myself to look again into the water.

A girl's face stared back up at me. Or was it only an illusion, created by the water and the mist? She blinked. She blinked again. She was alive!

Of course she's alive, I told myself. She's a girl; a live girl; a living, swimming girl. Big deal! You have a wild imagination.

But what was she doing there, anyway? And how had she gotten into the pool area so late?

It seems like she's been under a long time, I thought. A very long time. Too long. Maybe she needs help. Maybe she's . . . she is! She's drowning!

I panicked, cursing myself for not knowing how to swim. I had to run. Run for help. But I couldn't leave her, either. I had to help *now*.

She smiled at me then, still under the water, and raised her arm slowly. Not a call for help. More like a wave, an invitation. Was she okay? What was going on?

No, she's not okay, a voice inside me shouted. That's what happens when you drown. You go limp. You give up. She isn't okay. She isn't waving. She's drowning. She's dying. Do something!

"Don't give up," I commanded, knowing she couldn't hear. "Don't give up."

I scanned the balcony for a life ring, a rope, a pole. But there was nothing. I was about to scream, to call for help, when her head broke through the surface. I pressed against the railing, reaching down to her.

Wood cracked beneath me. The splash I made falling into the pool was the last sound I heard.

2

Churning water closed over me. It flowed into my mouth, choking me, scouring my throat, searing my lungs.

The girl of the water floated in front of me, serene, her long hair flowing around her like a curtain of gold. She gazed at me as if she knew me. And suddenly, everything was all right. She reached out to me. I stretched toward her. As our fingers touched, a tingle ran up my arm and through my whole body. Dazzling light danced on the surface of the water above me, and the girl was gone.

I was dead. I knew that. I reached toward the light. The light that would lead me away from the earth, away from my drowned body, lifeless now at the bottom of the pool. In the center of the light my father appeared. He laughed, his eyes crinkling, his arms open to me. So close. I kicked at the water and strained toward him. Almost there.

Suddenly I burst through the surface of the water and fell forward onto something hard and dry. I pulled myself forward, inch by inch, gulping air and clutching at rocks and weeds, terrified of slipping back into the water. Clinging to the earth, solid and safe beneath me, I blessed each stone and twig, wondering where they had come from, and how I had escaped death.

Or *if* I had.

The night was on fire. The whole sky, from horizon to horizon, was alive with blazing streamers of light. And there were flashes, some as large and brilliant as a full moon. The universe was coming apart at the seams.

Was I in heaven? Or hell? Or was I alive, but about to be incinerated in the holocaust that rained down? I ducked my head under my arms, waiting for that final flash of light and fire that would consume the world.

But the earth remained solid beneath me. And the sky, I suddenly realized, was quiet. I heard no thunderous explosions, was rocked by no shock wave concussions, felt no searing heat. If this was the end of the world, it wasn't what I had expected.

I forced one eye open a little. Through the narrow slit I saw only a few flashes of light. Not so threatening. Taken one or two at a time they looked familiar, like — my mind rushed back what seemed a million years, to the balcony, and shooting stars — the meteor shower!

I opened both eyes then, and slowly took my hands away from my face. Shooting stars fell like a blizzard. Hundreds and hundreds at once. Thousands, maybe. Uncountable meteors, rushing across the sky like a gigantic, soundless fireworks display. One brief glance and I was sucked upward, flung amidst meteors masquerading as stars, losing myself. Finding myself.

I collapsed onto my back, drunk with the light. Safe, in the middle of the universe.

A steady, soft brightness crept into the sky, the pale dawn tracing a horizon of hills around a vast meadow. Meteors, their brilliance dimmed by the coming day, still flashed notice of their brief lives.

I moved slowly, as if waking from a trance. Memory trickled in. Didn't I fall into the swimming pool? I touched my robe. It was dry. Where am I? Where is the Lodge? And how did I get to this wilderness?

There was no one in sight. Not a sign of civilization — no buildings, no roads, no street lights. Just an open, nearly treeless meadow stretching before me. Leading where? To what? The hills on the other side? And then where? More empty meadows, more uninhabited hills? My hands shook as I pulled my robe tighter around me.

That's when I heard it.

In all that barrenness, in all that quiet, someone cried out. Then whimpered. Someone in trouble. It sounded like a child, somewhere above me. Goose bumps sprouted on my arms. A cold lump of fear settled in my gut. In the half light, afraid to trust my body in this alien place, I crawled toward the sounds. I had to find this child, lost and alone. Like me.

I scrambled over sharp bushy things, up a steep incline, grasping for hand and footholds, my mind and my body reaching upwards. The whimpering was less intense now, less urgent. "It's all right," I whispered into the gloom. "I'll find you." Falling stars glinted intermittently overhead. "You're not alone." Like the trails of the meteors, my voice evaporated in the stillness.

11

Clutching at stones and tiny bushes, I inched up the steep slope. No more crying now. Did this child exist or was it my imagination? Was I all alone in my nightmare? A rock slid out from under my right foot. My shin landed on something hard. I rubbed my aching leg and wished I were safe in bed. Even the one at the Lodge, the bed from which I thought I had escaped my nightmare. Only to enter another.

"Papa. Papa."

The voice was tiny, and it came from just above me, where a rock ledge jutted out several feet from the hillside. I forgot the pain in my leg, scrambled up the last rise, and peered over the lip of the outcropping. At the edge of the flat rock a child of about four lay fast asleep on her side, arms wrapped around herself against the chill morning air.

"Papa," she called again in her sleep. As I pulled myself onto the ledge she woke with a cry.

"It's okay," I said as gently as I could. "It's okay."

She sat up, wiping at her scratched face, a quizzical yet trusting look in her hazel-green eyes. Her dress, cut like a gown in an old TV western, was torn and dirty.

"Don't move, honey. I'll come and get you. Everything's going to be all right." I scooted toward her. "We'll find your mama and papa."

She stuck a thumb into her mouth while the other hand pulled at a twig tangled in her long and curly blond hair. By the time I reached her she seemed more curious than frightened. Her tears were gone.

"How did you get here?" I asked.

She pointed up the hillside. "Fell," she said.

"But where's your mother and father? Where's mama and papa?"

"I don't know." A few faded, frantic meteors rocketed toward the horizon. She looked as if she might cry again. "The stars are falling," she whispered. She huddled against my side and hid her face in my neck.

"No, no," I said. "The stars aren't falling." But I didn't know how to explain meteors to such a young child. I could only hold her close and rock gently, her heart thumping hard next to mine.

Maybe I dozed for a moment. When I awoke I thought I heard horses whinnying. And deep, singsong voices; a kind of far-off chanting, like the whisper of breeze on a summer morning. But it wasn't a summer morning. It was cold, and the sky had gone crazy. Without this little girl scrunched into my side, needing me to take care of her, I would have collapsed from the sheer strangeness of it all.

The sounds stopped. Or maybe they had never really been. I stroked the little girl's hair and rocked her, crooning some nameless melody my mother had sung to me when I was about her age. It comforted me now, as it had then. The sun crept over a hilltop, and the girl fell asleep across my lap, her head in the crook of my arm. Her face was beautiful in that open, vulnerable way only a sleeping child's can be. I wished I had a little sister like her.

The pungent smell of sulphur pricked my nostrils. The same rotten egg smell as at the Lodge. I studied our surroundings. A small pool of steaming water edged with

13

grassy banks lay at the bottom of the hill. The very pool I had pulled myself out of — when? Last night? A river, narrow and wild, snaked through the valley, the color of its water changing from turquoise to frothy white in its rush over boulders.

Some things about the hills were familiar — their rocky silhouette, their reddish tint, the snow-covered mountain peaks rising behind them to the east. If I imagined the Lodge in front of me and the highway next to the river, it reminded me of Indian Springs valley.

But it couldn't be. This valley was swept clean of all traces of modern civilization. It was home only to sagebrush and bursting milkweed and waist-high russet grasses.

The meteors had faded entirely now, surrendering to the brightness of the morning sun. The child wiggled in my arms, groaned, and woke. The green of her eyes held a secret, a mystery I couldn't fathom. For a moment, a smile of contentment played across her face. Then it vanished, and a tear sprang from her eye. My heart ached for her, and for a loss I couldn't place, until she named it.

"Papa," she called.

"We'll find him," I promised again. I looked out over the valley, wondering where in all this wilderness to begin to look.

I saw the teepees for the first time then, a dozen or more tucked together at the base of the nearest hill. I gasped as if I'd been kicked in the chest.

I forced a deep breath. I wanted to believe this was all a dream. It had to be — except for this little girl, so real in my arms. I hugged her to me, felt the beat of her heart again, the warmth of her breath on my neck. She was no dream.

From our high perch I saw someone coming toward us from the teepees, a woman of dark skin and hair. She was wearing a long, light-colored dress, fringed at the bottom and along the sleeves, which covered her from neck to mid-calf. She moved quickly, efficiently, not so much walking as flowing over the earth, like wind in tall grass. Gentle, smooth, and knowing. She was heading straight toward us.

The little girl saw her, too. She sat up, eyes fixed on the mysterious apparition. "Indian lady," she said. And with no understanding of how it could be so, I knew that she was right. I waved at the woman, feeling strangely certain she could help. And would.

I felt a little hand groping for mine. I enfolded it in my own, and the sky swirled. The ledge quaked beneath me. I was falling.

3

Bright sunlight slapped me in the face. How could I have let myself fall asleep? Instinctively, I reached for the little girl. She was gone.

"There you are."

I jerked around. Sandy stood in a doorway, hands on hips, looking down at me.

"When I couldn't find you in your room I got worried. What are you doing out here, Lisa?"

I was on the balcony. Lying on the balcony in my night clothes. Had I been here all night? And what a dream! Images of the spirit of the water, the lost girl with the beautiful smile and long golden hair, the teepees, the mysterious woman, rushed through my fuzzy brain.

"Lisa, I don't know what this is all about, but you're in your pajamas in a public place and people are starting to go down to breakfast," she said, scouting the hallway behind her. "How long have you been out here, anyway?"

I sat up, taking in the balcony, the pool below, the sun already well above the hills. "I came out to look at the meteors," I said.

"Look at meteors? When?"

"I don't know." I squinted at the sun. "There was a meteor shower last night, wasn't there?" I asked, trying to straighten out the tangle inside my head.

"Well, honey," her tone softened, "I guess they said something about it on the radio but that was — do you mean to say you've been out here all night?" She sounded genuinely worried.

"I guess I fell asleep watching it," I said. "I'm all right," I added. "Really."

"Lisa, that's not the point." She frowned, and I was sure there was plenty more to come. But I was wrong. "Come on," she said. "We don't want to be last in line at the chow wagon."

She was trying hard to get along — maybe harder than I deserved, by the looks of things — and I appreciated it. I pulled myself to my feet. "Did you see them?" I asked.

"See what?"

"The stars. The falling stars. Sandy, there were so many! It was like a blizzard!"

She looked at me doubtfully. "Didn't they say there could be as many as sixty per hour? That's only one every minute. Hardly a blizzard," she said.

"It was, though. At least, it seemed like it." I ran my hand through my hair. "I don't know, maybe I was dreaming."

"Probably." She took a step toward the door. "Coming?"

"In a minute."

She looked at me as if I were a sick child.

"Really," I promised.

She nodded, then closed the balcony door behind her.

Was it a dream, I wondered? I had stepped out onto the balcony around midnight, watched some shooting stars, had those awful thoughts about Dad, then saw the face, the girl in the pool. My head resounded with that terrifying *crack* of splintering wood I'd heard as the railing gave way.

I hurried around the corner to the spot where I stood last night. My heart jumped. The rail was broken outward, its jagged edges extending over the water's glassy surface. I edged closer and looked down into the pool.

So quiet. And empty.

We ate in the outdoor cafe adjacent to the pool. Correction: Sandy ate. According to her, though, I merely "nibbled like a bird." I wore my swim suit under my clothes so that after breakfast I could sit by the pool and, as Sandy urged, make some friends for a change.

Sandy stirred her tea. "Any more nightmares?" she asked.

"No," I said quickly. I stared into my plate, searching among the crumbs for the real answer to that question.

"Hmm. Maybe balcony sleeping suits you," she said.

"Very funny."

It *was* kind of funny, to be honest, especially coming from Sandy, who is not one of the world's great kidders. But I didn't want to laugh. For one thing it felt too much like laughing at my nightmares, which were no joke at all. And it seemed, too, like a laugh would be letting her win something, although I didn't know what. I wasn't even sure if we were fighting. Or why. I just wanted to be alone.

"You look tired, actually," Sandy said. "Why don't you take a nap this afternoon? I'm going to finish my tea and then check on our house." She scrutinized me over the rim of her cup. "Don't scowl like that, Lisa. You'll like it once we get moved in. It's got high ceilings and leaded glass."

Old, I thought.

"And history."

Make that ancient.

"I like that it's not downtown," she said. "You know, room to breathe."

Will a four-wheel drive do, or will we need pack mules?

"And guess what? It's not far from the high school. You can walk!"

Great, I thought. I'll feel like I'm at school all the time. I had to get away from her before I either laughed or cried.

I wandered over to some deck chairs and lounges by the pool, deliberately passing under the balcony on the way. I looked up, searching for the broken railing, but couldn't find it. There was no splintered wood, no sign of damage. Everything looks perfectly normal, I thought. So what did I see this morning? An hallucination? Another dream? Maybe Sandy's right. Maybe I spend too much time alone. Maybe I *do* need some friends.

I flopped onto the nearest lounge chair to think. Wrong balcony, maybe. But a quick glance showed me there were no other balconies bulging off the Lodge. That was the one, and the railing wasn't broken.

I could see Sandy was keeping an eye on me. I took off my jeans and shirt, like a regular sunbather. I didn't need her coming over to find out what was "wrong." In my hurry I bumped my leg against the arm of the chair. The pain was surprisingly sharp. And when I rubbed it, my shin was sore to the touch. I was shocked to see a discolored bruise the size of a quarter on my shin.

. . . climbing a rocky hill in the half light of early morning. My foot slips and I come down hard on my shin . . .

But that was a dream, I reminded myself. You can't get a bruise from a dream.

I was standing there by the pool, probably gawking like an idiot, my jeans crumpled at my feet, trying to figure it all out. Fortunately, Sandy had left. The only person nearby was a bronze-skinned guy of about seventeen or eighteen sitting in one of the chairs, staring off into the rusty hills.

I settled back into my chair and within a few seconds was alternating between dozing and wondering about the little girl on the ledge. Is she all right? Did she find her papa? What if it wasn't a dream? My leg throbbed.

"Better be careful or you'll soon be redder than the hills around here."

I jolted to full consciousness at the sound of the unfamiliar voice.

"So what's it to you?" I snapped reflexively. I looked up into the brilliant blue eyes of Bronze-skin. It hadn't quite registered before: He was beautiful.

"I'm just saying, you're going to burn." He shrugged and started to walk away.

"Wait," I said, jumping to my feet. He stopped and turned. Great. Now what was I going to do? "Sorry," I said. "My mother's been on my case lately. Makes me mad. Sorry I took it out on you." I could hardly believe I was telling him all this. Some guy I didn't even know.

"Okay," he said. "You're forgiven. But I still think you should get out of the sun." We stepped into the shade of the Lodge and sat on the grass. "At this altitude the atmosphere is thin and the sunlight penetrates."

His voice was melodious, deep, and with a different rhythm than I was used to hearing.

"Have you lived here long?" I asked, trying to make brilliant conversation.

"Depends on what you think of as long. All my life, anyway." He smiled and ran a long-fingered hand through raven-black hair.

"I just moved to town and . . ."

. . . the Indian woman glides toward us through the tall grass . . .

". . . I was wondering, what kind of Indians used to live around here?" I asked. He cocked his head. "I'm kind of interested in history. My father teaches . . . taught it . . . I guess it rubbed off on me a little."

"Ute."

The sound, or word, meant nothing to me. "What?"

21

"Ute. Ute Indians."

"Ute Indians?"

"You've never heard of them," he said. I shook my head in agreement. "I'm not surprised. Utes lived all through the Shining Mountains. Up to a hundred years ago. Now . . . there aren't so many left."

"What are shining mountains?" I asked.

"It was our name for this part of the Rockies."

"Are you Indian?" I asked.

"My grandmother was full-blooded Ute."

"That's great," I said.

He studied me for a moment. "Are you white?" he asked.

"Yeah. Why?" I asked.

"That's great," he said, in the same tone I had used.

Why was he mocking me?

"Look," he said quietly, "having a full-blooded Ute grandmother isn't 'great.' Indians aren't 'great,' or 'good,' or 'bad,' — we're not some big homogeneous group. We're people. Same as you. Same as anybody. Calling us 'great' just makes us a curiosity, a dying species. Or it's a way to soften the guilt: We gave the Indians a bad deal. How can we make up for it? Let's say they're great. Let's say they're noble. Let's get out our camera and get a picture of one. Pay him a dollar, poor guy. Help him out."

"I didn't mean any offense," I said.

"I know," he said. "You didn't mean it, but it's offensive just the same. Sometimes it just gets to me. I didn't mean to give you a hard time."

"I know you didn't mean to," I said, "but . . ."

"I did anyway, didn't I?"

I nodded.

"Maybe we should start over," he said.

"Okay."

He extended his hand. "My name's Jay," he said.

"Lisa."

We shook hands.

"I'm hungry, Lisa. How about you?"

"Sure," I pretended. This is going better already, I thought.

We got snacks at the refreshment counter and sat at one of the tables in the shade of the huge old lodge building. Jay told me that the Utes had lived here for a thousand years. At least. The Shining Mountains were their beautiful home and provided for all their needs. They roamed them freely, from the highest passes to the grassy valleys below. They drank from the pure, cold streams and bathed in the hot springs, these very springs, when they returned from winter camp. Until the whites came.

. . . I rock her gently. A small pool of steaming water lies at the bottom of the hill . . .

"These springs are sacred for Nuu-ci," Jay said.

"New chee?"

"It means the People. Jay told me about his Ute grandmother, who died last spring. And how, since graduating in June — he had skipped a grade and was barely seventeen — he was trying to learn more about his Ute heritage.

Talking to Jay was sending tingles of excitement and fear pulsing through me. I'd never felt this way about a boy before, and we had only just met a few minutes ago. Part of me wanted to look into his eyes and talk for hours. Another part wanted to get up and run away.

On a sudden impulse I blurted, "Would you help me do some research on the Utes? I'd like to learn more about them. Their history, their way of life."

"Which way of life? During the Folsom Period? The horse period? On the reservations?" He was both teasing and serious now.

"Okay, okay. So hold your Folsom horses. I said I didn't know much about them. And anyway, I get your point."

"You do?"

"Well, yeah," I bluffed. "You're saying that . . . that people aren't all the same, and they don't always stay the same, either. Times change."

"People change."

"Everything changes."

"You know, that's pretty good," he said. "Maybe you got my point even better than I did. Life is change." He stood up, throwing his towel over his shoulder. "Got to get to work," he said.

I stood, too, facing him squarely. "Would you, though?" I asked.

"What?"

"Help me?"

I was thrilled when he agreed. We made a plan to meet at the library the next day at ten. I watched him walk away, light and swift, surefooted as a dancer.

Not an hour later Sandy broke the bad news: The house was ready. She would need my help moving all day tomorrow.

4

With a dreamy smile on her face, Sandy plopped down on a packing case on the front porch of the old house. "Won't this be great on hot summer evenings? We'll put a couple of chairs out here," she said, her voice rising with excitement, "or a porch swing." She saw my frown and her smile vanished. I felt like a jerk for ruining the moment, but I wasn't looking forward to rocking my life away on her beloved old porch. "Let's go in," she said.

I trudged in after her. Fresh paint. Boxes and furniture scattered around the living and dining rooms. Our new couch and dining set, out of place on the worn hardwood floors of the boxy rooms.

A window seat stretched from one wall of the dining room to the other, running under a large picture window flanked by narrow panels of etched and leaded glass. I sat on the hard wooden seat. From the house's high perch on Mountain Avenue I could see far beyond the immediate hills, mountains themselves by Missouri standards, to the distant profile of rugged grey-white peaks that formed the Continental Divide. Less than a mile from where I sat, the red tile roof of the Hot Springs Lodge peeked through the tree tops. Just beyond it, in the middle ground, the river and meadow stretched to the upsweep of the red clay hills.

... It is early morning. A child sleeps in my lap, while in the meadow by the river a Ute woman leaves the circle of teepees ...

Ute woman? Where had that idea come from? Probably the power of suggestion, from my talk with Jay.

"Lisa, come see the bedrooms," Sandy called from the kitchen. "The movers put my bed in the room off the dining room and yours in the one off the kitchen. But we can change it if you like."

I glanced into each bedroom. They were exactly alike. Small, plain, one large double-hung window. "It doesn't matter to me." I snuck a quick look at my watch. Ten o'clock already. "Sandy, can I take a break for awhile? I want to go over to the library."

"Take a break? You haven't done anything yet." She waved her hand toward boxes stacked halfway to the ceiling in every corner. "I start work tomorrow morning, Lisa. I can't do all this by myself."

End of discussion. Well, what was the point anyhow? It was after ten. Jay was waiting. Should I explain to Sandy that I wanted to meet someone? I knew how that would go: Oh? Who? Jay. Yes, Sandy, a boy. It's no big deal. No, I don't know his last name. Or where he lives. How old? Seventeen. He's smart. Graduated in June. A little old for me? He probably thinks so, too. But, you see, his grandmother was full-blooded Ute. And since I found the little girl the other night near the Ute camp by the river — that was after I saw the spirit in the pool, fell in and drowned, of course — I've had an overwhelming urge to find out more about these people. And Jay said he would help. Besides, he's really cute.

Wisdom, or maybe it was cowardice, got the better of me. I kept quiet and busied myself unpacking dishes. Sandy probably thought I was finally getting into the swing of things. But my thoughts were about Jay, wondering if he'd be mad at me and how I could find him tomorrow to explain. The only places I knew to look were the pool and the library. I didn't have a clue where he worked or lived, or even what his last name was.

We slaved through lunch, putting away kitchen supplies and all those closet things you don't know you have until you move. About three o'clock Sandy said she would walk over to the small store a few blocks away to get some food.

"Why don't you take a break. I'll be back in half an hour or so," she said.

I was exhausted, hot, and hungry. "Bring me some —"

"Fruit," she finished the sentence for me. I love fruit. And Sandy knows it.

While she was gone, I wandered around trying to recognize our stuff in this old, worn out house. I heard every creak of every floorboard. Kind of spooky, even in broad daylight. I pushed through the swinging door into the kitchen. Freshly painted yellow walls, their color intensified by the afternoon sun splashing through the large south window, greeted me like an old friend. Our kitchen at home was the same color. I was glad my bedroom was off this fiercely bright room after all.

28

As I entered the bedroom, I said, "My room" aloud, claiming it from its previous inhabitant. I put my clothes away in the chest of drawers and the small, dark cave of a closet, set up my desk under the window, and stacked my books on the built-in bookshelves. Four cartons of books, all that remained of Dad's collection — all that Sandy would pay to ship — had been stacked head-high in one corner by the movers. There they would stay, a shadow of my father, watching over me.

"I'm here," Sandy called as she came in the back door, "bearing many gifts of the edible variety." I joined her in the kitchen. "First, for the tired and hungry unpacking crew, we have sparkling cider. Then, everything needed for the creation of a superb and flavorful salad. Fruit salad, of course." She unloaded bananas, apples, large purple grapes, oranges, frozen strawberries, pears, a melon, and a pint of red raspberries so big I could fit them, like hairy thimbles, over the tip of my forefinger. "And," she held her nose, tossing the white-paper packaging to the side while she dangled a slab of filleted fish between her fingers, "*Monsieur Roughy D'Orange!*"

She had apparently mutated into a French chef. Despite her pantomimed disdain, she really did love fish. Would have had us eating it every night if Dad and I let her. I'd forgotten how much fun she could be when she let go. I had the feeling it was even going to taste good.

After eating and cleaning up I showered and, though it was only eight o'clock, snuggled into bed. The sounds, smells, and shadows of the house were alien, but at least

I was back in my own bed. I fell asleep almost immediately.

Sunlight streamed through my window. I lay in bed, listening to Sandy in the kitchen. The smell of coffee and toast wafted in. I felt cozy and warm all over. Safe. Like when I was a kid. The only thing missing was the sound of my parents talking quietly over their breakfast, solving all of life's problems for me before my feet touched the floor.

I got my own breakfast — leftover fruit salad. We ate without saying much. While Sandy got ready for work, I cleaned up the dishes. I promised to get some exercise at the pool and to pick up some more food afterwards at the little market.

"Try to meet some people," she counseled, heading toward the front door. "Don't spend what little time you have left before school starts sitting at home or at the library with your nose in a book."

It always seemed to me that Sandy had a fear of my love of books. She got nourishment out of running to meetings and spending time with friends. It bothered her that I didn't have friends to do things with.

I did have friends, kind of, but they were at-school friends. I went to a small, private, girls' school in St. Louis, with kids who came from all over the city. The bell rang at three and we got on buses or in our parents' cars and didn't see each other until seven forty-five the next morning. I learned to do without friends. Which was just as well, because now they were all a thousand miles away.

The way I saw it, I was lucky I *could* get my nourishment from books. Books are not people. You don't have to leave books. And they don't leave you.

5

The pool was jammed with kids. I had walked around the perimeter four times looking for Jay. He wasn't there. I was heading toward the exit when I heard it.

"You're not leaving, are you?"

A very tall, very thin, and very red-haired girl loomed over me. Before I could answer, she said, "My name's Geneva. You know, as in Switzerland."

"I'm sorry —" I was about to tell her I had to go.

"No need," she interrupted. "It's an unusual name, but I'm used to it." Her eyes were large and tawny. "You can call me Genny for short."

She grinned and a thousand freckles grinned with her.

"Get it? Genny for *short*. Now if I could just get a figure to match my height," — she stretched as tall as she could and strutted a few steps like a model on a runway — "dahlink, I coold be in piktoors," she said, mugging the steamy look on the cover of every romance novel.

Sudden as lightning she returned to normal and said, "I'm fifteen. How old are you?"

"Fifteen," I said.

"Are you a sophomore?"

"Yes."

"Great. We'll be in the same classes. In fact, my friend Michael — he's on a trip right now, but he'll be back when school starts — he's a sophomore, too."

"What makes you think I'm going to school here? How do you know I'm not a tourist?"

She closed her eyes and put her hand to her forehead in a mock trance. "Message cumss to me," she said in an exaggerated accent that could only belong to someone from Everywhere. "It sehss theht you are movink into haussa on zee street uff zee mountains. Yesterdeh, no?"

"How do you know that?" I asked, struggling to keep a straight face.

"Iss small town, Miss Carey. Also, am livink down zee block from you." She snapped her eyes open, turned the accent off, and peered at me through binocular-shaped hands. "I saw you and your mom move in."

"So how do you know my name?"

"What? You want all my secrets?" she protested. "Okay. My dad works in the accounting department at the college, same as your mom. I think he met her when she came over to find her office or something. When he saw her moving in so close, he said he would talk to her about carpooling. Your mom's so young! You look like sisters. Well, anyway," she bulldozed on, "we could walk to school together. Springs High is only about six blocks."

I nodded. Genny breathed. This girl's motor was running a little too fast for me.

"Listen, I've got to be going, Gen—"

"Know how I got that name? I was born there."

"What?"

33

"Not what. Where. Geneva. Switzerland. I was born there. Hence, Geneva."

"Lucky you weren't born in Krakow," I said.

She doubled up, laughing. I had to admit, Geneva-from-Switzerland did intrigue me, but I had this horrible suspicion that Sandy had set up this little meeting for my benefit. And, in any case, I needed a breather.

"See you later, Geneva," I said, and walked out the exit. She followed. "Genny," she said.

"Pardon?"

"Call me Genny," she said.

"Genny. Right."

"Where are you off to?" she asked, falling in step beside me. This girl isn't shy, I concluded. Or maybe she's playing the part my mother wrote for her.

"To the library," I said, turning down the sidewalk.

"Wrong way."

"Oh."

"I'll show you."

Oh no.

"Just tell me where it is. I'll find it."

"That's all right," she said, all graciousness. "I want to go anyway. *À la bibliothèque.*"

"*O! Parlez-vous Français?*" I replied, trying to be friendly.

"Uh, no. I mean, just a little," she said bringing her thumb and forefinger so close they almost touched.

"*Moi, aussi.* Did you learn French in Switzerland?" I asked.

"No, I learned it in French class," she said. "My dad packed us up and moved us back to the States when I didn't speak anything but goo-goo and gah-gah. I was a wee lassie." She made an attempt at a Scottish accent.

"So are you Swiss or French or Scottish or what?" I asked a little peevishly, though she hadn't done anything to deserve it.

"American. Swiss. Both."

"What about your mother?"

"What about her?"

"Is she from Geneva?"

"No."

"She doesn't live with you, huh?"

"What makes you say that?"

"Well, you said 'my dad packed us up.'"

"Oh. Yeah. She died."

"Oh, I'm sorry," I said. I felt awful.

"No need. It was almost right after I was born. An avalanche. I didn't even know her." She shrugged as if it didn't matter, but the corners of her mouth kind of drooped and she looked away as she said it. "Lots of water's gone down the old Rhône since then."

I pulled the apple and banana I brought for lunch out of a brown paper sack and offered them to Genny. She picked the apple and ate it, noisily, the rest of the way.

The library turned out to be an ancient stone building. Inside it smelled kind of like my old elementary school — floor cleaner and furniture polish mingled with a general mustiness. Seconds after our entry it was clear to me that this was unexplored territory to Genny. But it was a tiny

35

place and within a minute I'd brought us to a special case called the Colorado Shelf, which included books on Colorado history. I hoped there would be something about Utes. Genny hung over my shoulder as I studied the titles.

"Whatcha lookin' for?" she asked.

"Nothing." I wanted to keep my interest in local Native American history to myself or, better yet, between Jay and me. "I like to read about the history of places I visit."

"You mean *live*, don't you?"

"Yes," I agreed. "Live. Unfortunately."

"Hey, don't complain. I've lived so many different places, it was always *like* visiting. From Geneva to San Francisco to Baltimore. Sometimes for just a few months. I never paid much attention to the history. The last place we lived, which was Baltimore, I spent all my time at Harborplace — boat rides, the National Aquarium, tons of great food, and lots of guys sunbathing on sailboats all over the place . . ."

Genny was off and running like the horses at the Preakness, which she told me was a big horse race in Baltimore. She had apparently never heard of the custom of keeping quiet in a library. When she finally went off to find a bathroom, I grabbed five books off the Colorado Shelf — anything with the word "Ute" in the title. Then I looked around for Jay.

My search didn't take long. There was only one room on the main floor. I rushed through the stacks, finding only an older couple browsing through magazines. Then down a stairway to the basement, which turned out to be the children's area — elfin tables and chairs, half a dozen kids to match. How was I ever going to find Jay? Was he a dream, too?

When I got back upstairs, Genny was tapping her foot and looking around, her red hair swishing on her back.

"Where have you been?" she asked anxiously.

"Just looking at the rest of the library."

"Not much to it, *n'est-ce pas?*"

"That's for sure."

I grabbed a few books at random from the New Fiction Shelf, just so Genny wouldn't notice all the Ute titles.

"Kind of particular, aren't you?" she quipped.

I wished I could pull up a chair, start reading, and watch for Jay, but I knew that would be impossible with Genny anywhere within a mile. I suggested we walk home and she quickly agreed. She hadn't picked out any books and I wondered again if she had only come with me because Sandy had somehow wheedled her into taking care of me. I got a library card and checked my books out, watching with alarm as Genny stuffed them into her backpack.

"You read a lot, *oui*?" she asked as we stepped out into bright sunshine. As usual, I was barely able to nod before she continued. "I never got the habit, what with moving so often. I had more important things to do. Like finding my way around, seeing the sights, and trying to make friends. I saw a lot of sights, but friends take more time. Just about when I would start to get to know a few people — bam! — packing time again. But Dad promised we'd stay here in Indian Springs at least until I graduate." She

37

frowned. "I hope he realizes that's three whole years. That'll be the longest I've ever lived anywhere."

She stopped suddenly and grabbed my hand, pulling me to an abrupt halt. "You know, I think he's been running away from something," she whispered. It seemed like another one of her acts, but a quick look into her eyes told me she was serious. I nodded, feeling uncomfortable, and not really knowing what to say.

When we got to her house I noticed a handwritten card on the side of the old mailbox at the curb. "John Smith" it read. "Geneva Smith" was written under that. A wide strip of clear tape fastened the card to the box and protected it from rain. Above the card, on the grey box itself, names had been scraped off.

"Who was that?" I asked, pointing to the unreadable names.

"My Gramp and Grannie," Genny said. "They died, both of them, last year, just a few months apart." She traced what I supposed was her grandmother's name with a long, pink finger. "They were the best," she said.

A second later she was pulling me up the walk.

"Come see my room!" she said.

It was incredible. Jammed with stuffed animals, posters, a parakeet cage, a huge aquarium, and two large orange cats asleep on the bed. *Gurgling* and *chirping* nearly drowned out everything she said.

"This is the room I always used when I visited Gramps and Grannie. My dad told me I could have a pet when we settled down for awhile. And now that we have — *voila!* Since we moved here in June I've found a few friends."

That seemed an understatement. And not only had she found them, she'd named them. First and last names. Everybody, even the fish. She called the cats the Beer brothers, Ginger and Root. The parakeets were Ralph and Abernathy.

Finally, after she made me repeat all their names — including hers, Genny Magdalena Smith — and I promised to come back soon, I was allowed to retrieve my books from her pack and leave. She came to the door with me.

"I have to clean the aquarium and then make dinner or I'd come to see your room," she said.

"Another time would be better," I answered. "It's not ready yet."

But there was more to it than that. Here was a girl who had lost her mother practically at birth, whose body had so far grown very tall and little else, and who, through no fault of her own, had never had a chance to have a real friend. Yet she was vivacious, self-confident, had a terrific sense of humor, and was able and willing, it appeared, to reach out to new people at the drop of a hat.

Our rooms said it all. Mine was a spartan cell, a table set for one. Genny's was a lavish hall, a Thanksgiving feast with guests and all the trimmings.

I felt more alone than I ever had in my life.

6

"Long ago," I read, "a man dreamed that he should go to a certain place in the mountains. He knew it was a sacred dream, and that he must do as it instructed him. And there, in that place that he dreamed about, he saw a bear coming out of hibernation. The bear shuffled back and forth, back and forth, in a dance-like motion. The bear taught the man the dance and the man taught the People.

"Each spring the People danced the Bear Dance to honor the bear and to welcome the coming of new life. They built a large corral out of cedar branches. Women chose their partners and led the men into the center of the corral where the back and forth shuffling of the Bear Dance lasted for three to four days.

"The dance started slowly, but by the last day became faster and more intimate. Some couples became lifelong mates after the Bear Dance . . ."

"Lisa!"

Sandy? Already? I didn't even hear her come in.

"Where'd you hide the groceries?" she asked.

Oh, no. I'd forgotten to go shopping. Not forgotten, really. Just gotten so wrapped up in one of my books that I'd lost track of time. I tossed the book back onto the pile.

"Sorry," I said as I entered the kitchen. "I'll go to the store right now. I was —"

"Reading, I'll bet" Sandy said. "Can't you ever take my advice? You never meet people or do anything but read."

"Well, you're wrong. I went to the pool. I met someone."

"Who?"

As if she didn't know.

"Geneva Smith." I waited for a look of recognition. Nothing. "Smith. You know, the man you work with? Who also happens to live on this street?"

"John Smith?"

"That's what it says on his mailbox."

"I didn't know he had a daughter. What did you say her name is?"

She didn't have that glint in her eyes like when she's plotting a better life for me. She really didn't know.

"Geneva," I repeated meekly.

"Geneva," Sandy said, testing the sound. "Well, I'm glad you've made a friend." Calling her a friend was going a bit far and I was about to say so when Sandy volunteered, "Why don't I go to the store and get something for supper."

"No. Let me. I promised."

"Okay. But hurry. I'm hungry already."

And so I went, even though what I wanted to do more than anything was to get back to my book. "My little scholar," my father used to say. "Has to know everything about the subject she's latched onto. Drain it dry." Later, I promised myself.

Although the sign above the entrance read **REDPATH'S GENERAL STORE**, the interior was smaller than a convenience store. The aisles were narrow. The shelves reached all the way to the ceiling, sagging in places under the weight of the merchandise which jammed them. And they were made of real wood, the warm, honey-toned finish contrasting sharply with the gaudy brand-name packagings, a battle between the past and the present.

"He must go. Now."

The words startled me. It was a man's voice, urgent, and turned me instantly into an eavesdropper. I looked quickly around. The store seemed to be empty.

"Give him some space," a female voice answered. "He is not your uncle. He is not you."

I noticed a doorway at the back of the small store, covered by a heavy curtain.

"You're right, Marie. He's not my uncle. He's my *son*."

They had to be behind that curtain.

"*Our* son," she corrected. "And if he goes for you, or me, rather than for himself, that is doomed. Give him time to know his own heart."

"But if he doesn't go now, it may be too late. I've seen it —"

"James," she interrupted in a coarse whisper. "A customer."

I turned away from the curtain and fixed my eyes on the nearest shelf: bars of soap. I grabbed one and studied the package intently, hoping to pass for a serious comparison shopper.

The woman was beside me. "Hello," she said. "Anything I can help with?" She had ash-blond hair, bright blue eyes and a full figure. She looked older than my mother. Maybe forty-five.

"I don't think so," I said, just as the man emerged from behind the curtain and joined us. He was the same height and age as the woman but he was dark-skinned, with black eyes that lent intense energy to his otherwise calm face.

They introduced themselves as Marie and James Redpath, the owners of the store. Marie was very inquisitive. What was my name? Was I a new resident or on vacation? Where did I live? Finally they connected me to the "pretty young blonde" who had just moved in up the street.

"You remember. The fish lady," James said.

"How can that be?" Marie objected when I explained that Sandy's my mother. "She's too young to have a daughter in college."

"I'm in high school," I said.

She looked me up and down. "Sisters," she joked.

Nothing I hadn't heard before. There was a different feeling to their probing, though. It wasn't nosey. It was as if they were taking us in as friends, Sandy and I, people they already cared about and wanted to get to know better.

I grabbed a few items for supper. An old, green, metal register dominated the varnished pine counter. It chugged mechanically and coughed open its drawer to accept the crumpled bills I pulled from my wallet.

As I walked up Mountain Avenue toward home I wondered about what I had heard. Go where? Too late for *what*?

While Sandy cooked the spaghetti, I washed the green beans and asked about her first day at work. It was all the encouragement she needed. She talked about her new job through meal preparation and dinner and cleanup. I didn't miss the sparkle in her eyes as she told me that she and John Smith would be carpooling the two short miles to work.

After the dishes were put away, I was glad to get back to my room. The library books sat on my desk, beckoning to me like a treasure chest from the ocean floor. I slipped the top one off the stack and opened to the chapter on mineral hot springs.

The Utes journeyed to hot springs, it said, to cure illness or to ease away aches after the long cold winter. Of all the beauty and bounty of their Shining Mountains, hot springs were their greatest prizes. The springs here in town were especially cherished by the Utes, just as Jay had told me. They were considered to be a powerful source of healing, a holy place, where spirits lived.

. . . Churning water closes over me. It flows into my mouth, choking me . . . The girl of the water floats in front of me . . .

A sudden chill gripped me, one so violent that I could not stop trembling. I got into bed, clothes and all, and burrowed beneath the blankets, but the cold hardly lessened. Somehow I fell asleep.

... *The little girl's blond hair bounces wildly as she tries to keep step with the older dancers. Kaleidoscope figures swirl by, a dizzying series of browns, coppers, and golds. The moon is full. It is the Bear Dance.*

Suddenly the girl is no longer little. She is a young woman, her long golden hair swaying in time with the dance. Now the sky darkens, the corral shudders and seems to growl. The whole corral is falling, being pushed in. The growls grow into roars. The dancers' faces twist with terror as a great, humped grizzly slashes like furred lightning into their midst.

The woman is thrown to the ground by a gigantic paw. The moon turns blood red ...

I woke up sobbing, racking sobs that tore my throat and hurt my chest. Sandy sat beside me on the bed, massaging my back. She was in her nightgown. "It's all right. Everything's all right," she said gently over and over again.

I remembered my father, lying so still between the sterile, white hospital sheets. A separation I couldn't bear to think about was upon me then, but I had crowded it out and left his hospital room that night thinking only about his getting well. Coming back home. "Everything will be all right," I promised myself then. "Everything will be all right." Perhaps my body knew the truth. I was sick with chills and fever, and tormented by horrific dreams all that night. The phone rang early the next morning. They said we should come quickly. Back to the hospital. Back to the

45

room. When I entered I knew at once that he was not asleep, that he was not in a coma. No sleep, no coma, looks like death.

Sandy's hand was gentle on my back. "Everything's all right," she soothed again.

But everything wasn't all right. Nothing ever would be.

I was exhausted the next morning. My head ached, and someone had poured onion juice in my eyes while I slept. Sandy was tired, too. She dragged around the house, gulping cups of tea, trying to cheer me up by telling me what to do: eat dry toast, try an herbal tea, rest in bed until I felt better. Then go out and be with people. Maybe Geneva would be home to "play with."

"I'm not eight years old," I mumbled as she left for work.

The day was fuzzy, without the crisp edges and sense of security that a schedule, or at least a goal, provides. I lay in bed, nibbling an apple, thinking about my father, and the Bear Dance, and the little lost girl, and last night's nightmare. Strange how the mind works, bringing together reality and unreality, weaving a new dream fabric from remnants of both. I remembered reading somewhere how we might have it backwards, that dreams might be reality and waking life the dream. I tossed the minuscule apple core into the wastebasket and headed out the door for the Lodge. It was time to figure out what was going on.

Hordes of guests streamed like ants between the lobby and the pool entrance a hundred yards away. Despite my earlier fatigue I felt energized now and took the steps two at a time. Just outside the balcony doors an older couple sat in plastic-weave chairs, talking quietly. I hurried past, around the corner to the railing, and saw at once that it was in fact unbroken, good as new.

I ran my hand absently over the top rail, then the lower one, trying vainly to make some sense of things. While the logic gears in my brain spun uselessly, a message from my fingertips trickled in: The upper rail is smoother, they said. The upper rail is smoother. And when I looked where my fingers touched I noticed that it appeared a shinier white than the rail below. I put my nose close. Fresh paint.

Good as new, all right. It *is* new.

I leaned against the stout corner post that supported the balcony roof, my back to the din which rose from the pool below. A little lost girl, bears and Bear Dances. Dreams? Reality? I closed my eyes and in my mind's eye, too, daylight faded. The pool was empty, and the water swirled around like it had the other night.

My hand caressed the shiny new railing. I knew what I must do.

7

There was no doubt that Sandy was sleeping as I tiptoed past her bedroom door that night. Neither Dad nor I could ever convince her that she snores.

The night was cool, the sky clear as I walked down silent, empty streets to the Lodge. Every now and then a shooting star streaked across the stygian sky. One left a green trail that lingered for six or eight seconds. Like a memory.

I paused at the Lodge entrance to put on my yes-of-course-I'm-staying-here look, then grasped the ornate brass knob. It would not turn. I shoved at the door but it was rock solid. I stepped back, dumbfounded, when it burst open without warning, almost knocking me down. A couple swayed past.

"'Scuse me," the man proclaimed in a too-loud voice.

I hurried inside and scrambled up the stairs, missed my footing about half way up and caught myself in a three-point landing, like a figure skater after a bad leap. The desk clerk arched one lazy eyebrow over his tattered newspaper.

"Good night," I squeaked.

"Yeah," he said, shaking the limp paper to attention. I was home free.

The balcony door stood open. A warm breeze billowed through like the breath of an unseen giant. When I stepped across the threshold and out onto the balcony I had the eerie feeling that my life would never be the same again. I closed the door, separating myself from the rest of the world.

Wrapping my arm securely around the solid end post at the far corner of the balcony I looked down, half expecting — half hoping, really — to see the water girl. But there was nothing. For a long time I stared hard, trying to stab holes through the thick, drifting clouds of mist, but catching only passing glimpses of the water's glass-like surface. I struggled to call up images of the water nymph, but they would not come. The screen in my head was blank.

After a string of failed attempts, a shiver took me by surprise, ran up my spine and rattled my teeth. The damp night air was getting to me. I felt silly. I had been out here for who knows how long, acting like a kid who still believes in Santa Claus, trying to make magic happen. What would my father think of his little scholar if he could see me now?

I wondered if he *could* see me where he was. *If* he was. Another shiver rippled through me. Nightmare images started forming at the edges of my mind. I didn't want those awful pictures in my head again.

"Spirit. Spirit." I intoned the mantra, remembering the other night here on the balcony. "Spirit. Spirit."

And just like then, the water swirled beneath me. I felt dizzy and tightened my hold on the post. I scrunched my toes, trying to grip the balcony floor through my rubber soles. I wanted to take it back, take back the word that had somehow set this all in motion. But it was too late. What I had hoped for, happened.

The same face appeared through the mists. The same long, light hair undulated like waves in the water. Her soft eyes beckoned to me from out of a gossamer watercolor. The pull to join her was strong. I felt I had known her all my life and that to be with her now was the most important thing.

It went against my normal judgment, and logic raged at me as I climbed onto the railing. But I was listening to another voice, one less familiar but calm and wise, and which I trusted instinctively as it urged me onward. I knew that I was no marionette responding to the pull of invisible strings. The voice I followed came from inside. It was my own.

I balanced for a moment, my arm wrapped like a lifeline around the stout end post. And then I jumped.

An eternity passed as I plunged, weightless, through empty space. Then a solid smack, like a heavy board slapping the bottoms of my feet, and I was thankful I had not thought to remove my shoes. Instinctively I gulped air and pinched my nose tight with one hand as the rush of water ballooned my pant legs and bunched my shirt and jacket under my armpits.

At the last instant, as my head went under, I felt a rush of fear. But there was no time for regret. Water roared like a beast all around me, tearing at my hair as I knifed downward. In a moment my feet hit the concrete bottom and my legs accordioned beneath me. I opened my eyes.

Just a few feet above me, enveloped in a million bubbles, I saw the water girl. Gracefully, like an angel of mercy, she stretched her arms toward me. I grabbed at those arms like a drowning sailor flails at a passing timber.

A tingle shot through me. She was gone.

I lay on my side next to a small natural hot pool which belched sulfur fumes. The concrete pool was gone, as were the Lodge, the highway, the whole town. The electric lights of city living had been replaced by a full moon just above the horizon, yet so bright that every bush and tree cast a shadow. I had been here before.

Across from what should have been Hot Springs Drive a luminous sky shimmered above a cluster of bonfires. A circle of teepees squatted near the river's edge and, nearby, a line of evergreen trees I didn't remember, growing so close together they looked like a Christmas tree lot.

I had made it. And it seemed that the girl in the hot springs was the link. I ran through patches of snow toward the teepees, cold air washing my face and stinging my eyes. Luckily, my clothes were dry. Just like the last trip, I remembered. I was glad I had worn a jacket.

I stumbled, pitched forward, and landed on my hands and knees. Pulling myself up, I brushed off my clothes and took a moment to assess the situation. The obvious question was, What am I doing running toward a bunch of teepees in the middle of the night? Worse yet, in the middle of who knows where? And who knows when? If the darkness had swallowed me up then and deposited me safely back in my bed, with Sandy snoring away reassuringly in the next room, I would have been the last to object.

I turned back, lurching unsteadily as I retraced my steps through the matted grasses to the hot springs. My skin tingled with the feeling that I was being watched, that I might be grabbed at any moment by some unseen assailant and carried to the teepees as a captive. I reached the pool, in a darkness still crowded with eyes, and stepped into the shallow water.

Nothing happened.

"Okay," I said aloud to whoever guards the passageways between times. "I changed my mind. It's time for me to go back now. Back to cars and pollution and that ramshackle house." I waited. "Right now, please."

Still nothing.

The ledge. Last trip I had returned to my time from the ledge. Maybe that was the key. I scrambled over rocks up the steep hill, forgetting in my panic the narrow trail I had used to find the little girl. But there was no child this time. When I pulled myself onto the stone, I was alone.

The moon had crept a bit higher, so sharp and close in the thin, clean air that I could have reached out and touched it. The crisp scent of pine assailed my nostrils, reminding me that I had stood in this very spot only a few nights ago. But obviously more than a few nights had passed in this world. Then there had been no moon, now the moon was full. Had it been two weeks, or had many moons swollen and shrunk, or even many winters come and gone? And where was the little girl who once slept here in my arms? No answers. Only questions.

I studied the Ute settlement. Bonfires blazed. There was a lot of activity in the camp, but there was a kind of flow, too, a direction. And it was clearly toward the trees, which I now saw to be *cut* trees or bushes, lashed together to form a large, circular fence out in the meadow. Something important was happening.

And, oddly, I felt that it involved me. Sitting there on the rock I was struck by a sense that I had not only come back to this time or place or whatever it was for my own purpose — to find the little girl — but that I had been invited here. That I had not only pushed from my end, but had been pulled also from this. And that this particular night I had dropped myself into was not just a matter of chance.

I was at once excited and frightened, attracted and repelled. In the end, curiosity and a sense of purpose got the best of me. Once more I retraced my steps, dodging bushes and rocks across the moon-shadowed meadow, right up to the first teepee.

As if to greet me, a baby crawled out. I froze where I stood, in the shadow of a tree just a few steps away. He babbled, sucked on a pudgy finger, and paid no attention to me, as if he didn't see me, or as if I wasn't there. He crawled further from the teepee, then stopped again, not

53

five feet from me. I waved a hand in front of his face. He babbled some more, then started off in a new direction, still further from home, still ignoring me. Feeling bold, I jumped into his path, waved my arms and made a funny face. He kept crawling. He would have bumped into me if I hadn't darted out of the way. A moment later he sat down and cried.

My heart pounded as a young woman, dressed in beautiful buckskin dashed out of the teepee and rushed toward us. Cooing in soft, motherly tones she scooped him up. She looked casually around, her line of sight swinging right through me just a few steps away.

"Hello." My voice shook. "Your baby's really cute."

Without a sign that she had heard, she turned and carried her baby back to the teepee, disappearing through the small entry.

Exhilarated by my freedom, I wandered through the camp, right up to the entrance of the brush corral. Inside the large enclosure a series of ten or twelve small fires formed another, slightly smaller circle. Between the ring of brush and the ring of fire, lots of people were sitting. To the left of the entrance sat the women of the tribe. To the right were the men. The mood seemed festive yet charged with tension, like a balloon just before it bursts. Without warning, raspy growls erupted from somewhere past the empty middle of the arena, at the far side of the circle.

. . . the sky darkens, the corral shudders and seems to growl . . .

I stiffened. Was my dream about to come true?

Strong, masculine voices, some deep and guttural, some piercing and shrill, answered the invisible beast with a wailing chant. But, as their voices rose and fell, the growling grew louder and more rhythmic. Still, no one but me seemed afraid. And I noticed that all eyes were on a group of men across the corral from me.

There were seven of them, sitting shoulder to shoulder. Each held two white sticks, or maybe they were bones. One was deeply notched, like crocodile teeth, its far end pointed down and pushed against a hide stretched tight over what looked like a hollow log. Singing with abandon, each man rubbed the other stick up and down over the notches, creating the thundery, growling sound I heard.

Was this the Bear Dance? It fit the description I'd read about, and it fit my dream. But if it was, I hoped the only bear sounds to come that night would be from the instrument the singers played.

A woman strolled over to the men's side of the circle, flipped a fringe of her sleeve at one particular man, then walked to the center of the corral. She stood there alone for a few moments. The man she had indicated followed and stood facing her, a few steps separating them. Other women picked out their partners in similar ways.

Soon, two long lines, one of women and one of men, stood facing each other, bisecting the corral. Buckskin and beads, flesh and feathers, rocked in unison to the singers' song and the growling of the bones. The line of women moved forward two steps, then backwards three. The line of men followed like a mirror image, stepping back when the women moved forward, forward when the women stepped back. The lines of dancers moved together, back and forth, like an ocean wave. Or, maybe, like a bear coming out of hibernation.

But where was my little friend? She was not with the women on the sidelines, nor anywhere that I could see. I left the corral to look for her and came upon a man, standing alone, gazing at the moon. He was taller, more powerfully built, and redder in skin tone than the other men I'd seen. He looked about thirty years old. He seemed to be waiting for something. I watched him until I had the prickly gooseflesh feeling that my presence disturbed his thoughts. He looked around for a few moments then back to the moon. I hurried into the cluster of teepees.

Just about everyone was gone. The few who remained, mostly older adults and very young children, sauntered toward the circle of branches. I searched the faces and even some of the teepees looking for the little girl. No luck.

The sound of soft voices drew me toward two women talking by a nearby campfire. One was a girl about my age, with blond hair lying in waves on her shoulders. The woman with her was older, shorter, and much darker. The older woman was speaking. Her voice rose and fell like music, yet carried great authority. I was startled to notice that, although they spoke in a language my ears did not know, I seemed to hear inside my head a translation that I could fully understand.

"You have been my granddaughter for twelve winters," she told the girl. "A woman tonight, you will dance. I know whom you will choose. He is tall, strong, a brave hunter. He, too, was adopted by the People. He was a man ready to dance even when you came to us. But he waited for you to grow into a woman."

The younger woman stood still as a tree.

"He will bring deer to you. You will cook it and eat with him. And that is good. We will welcome him into our lodge."

The younger woman nodded solemnly. "Thank you, Grandmother," she said.

Grandmother's face was deeply wrinkled, yet the way she moved and held her body made me think of a younger woman. The girl hugged her lightly, as in a ceremony. Then she came toward me. I retreated, backing around the perimeter of the nearest teepee, but she seemed to pursue me.

"Why do you run away from me?" she asked quietly. I stopped, and she touched my shoulder. She could see me as well as I could see her. "Are you not my friend from the spirit world?" I nodded, more a reflex than an answer. "I have always known you would return. You have come back this night when I dance the Bear Dance."

. . . the corral shudders and seems to growl . . . The dancers' faces twist with terror as a great humped grizzly dives into their midst . . . The young woman is thrown to the ground by a gigantic paw . . .

Could this be the little girl I held on my lap only a few nights ago?

She obviously recognized me. I stared in shock at the little-girl-grown-up: the same long, blond hair, resting now on the shoulders of a woman. And I began to understand the weird paradox. Even though she hadn't seen me for twelve years, except for my change of clothes I looked exactly the same as I had the first time we met; even though I had seen her just a few nights ago, she had aged twelve years.

She was a few inches shorter than me, lithe yet solid and strong. Her skin was suntanned bronze and her buckskin dress a tawny white. Other than her hair and hazel-green eyes this young woman did not remind me at all of the frightened little girl on the ledge. She was confident and calm, and though only about my own age, ready tonight to choose a partner for life.

"You've been living with these people since we met on the ledge twelve years ago?" I asked.

"Yes," she said.

"Did you ever find your papa?"

"No."

She spoke these simple answers with a lack of emotion that startled me. Perhaps it showed in my face.

"Do not be sad for me," she said. "After you returned to the spirit world, Grandmother found me on the ledge. She and her daughter, my mother, raised me as their own. The People cherish their children. My life is good."

"How did your grandmother find you?" I asked.

"Leaves Always Green has great power and wisdom. She is a holy woman. She heard me call to her. So she came out from the camp. Then she saw you signal to her." She waved her arm in the air as I had that night. "She told me you left then because it was time for you to return to the spirit world."

58

"But I'm not from the spirit world. I think . . ." I hesitated a moment, trying to convince myself. ". . . I think I'm from the future."

She squinted at me, mystified. How could I explain?

But before I could try she said, "I dream about what will happen. That is the future you come from?" Her face wrinkled in concern.

"I don't know," I said. "What do you dream?"

"Square lodges, one after another in long lines." She was at a loss for words. With her hands she chopped the air back and forth. "Many people, most light of skin like me. Many, many." More chopping. "Large shiny animals moving fast, faster than our fastest horse. And loud." She covered her ears. "And many people." She shook her head, more in disbelief than in judgment. "Too many people, who do not look at one another. Much hurry. Too many." She held her hands palm down, dangling her slender fingers and wiggling them frantically, then looked at me. "Is this where you are from?"

The answer was obvious.

"Yes," I said. Now it was she who looked sad.

She looked off suddenly to one side and, following her gaze, I saw through a gap in the teepee cluster the tall man I had seen earlier. He turned his head toward us — toward her — and an invisible message seemed to pass between them. She smiled.

"I must go now," she said. "Will I see you again?"

The Bear Dance nightmare crowded its way back into my head. If this girl could dream something that she had no way of knowing, maybe I could, too.

"Don't go!" I exclaimed. "I have to tell you something."

"Then you must tell me now," she said, taking my hand in her own.

Growls from the corral surrounded me as I fell into blackness.

8

I pulled myself out of a cramped knot of discomfort and up off the hard floor of the Lodge balcony. I weighed at least a thousand pounds. I held my dew-coated right hand out in front of me, examining the back and palm as though I had never seen such an object before. Didn't she — it couldn't have been more than a few moments ago — didn't she just touch this hand?

Of one thing I was certain. What had happened over the course of the night was not a dream. Which left only two options: Either I was totally crazy, or I really had gone back in time, back to see the little girl grown up, ready to dance the Bear Dance with her chosen life partner.

But what about my Bear Dance nightmare from night before last, I asked myself? Despite the crisp morning air my body went hot with fear as I replayed the scene in my mind. Was it a mere coincidence that I should dream about a Bear Dance and then time travel to what might be that very event? How could traveling in time even happen, much less be coincident with anything? Can nightmares come true? Was mine a warning? I'd never had dreams that predicted the future. Of course, what happened to the girl wasn't really the future at all. It was the past. Could my nightmare somehow recall the past, like hers had somehow foreseen the future? My brain burned as I tried to sort it all out.

It was light, but the sun had not yet risen as I moved noiselessly down the stairs and out the Lodge exit. I wished I could get in touch with Jay. I wanted to tell him about what was happening and see if he could help me fill in the blanks. But I discarded that idea. He'd think I was nuts. Who wouldn't?

Still, something deep in my center told me that whatever this was about, it was important. I felt as though I were on a journey, going somewhere exciting, yet without knowing what the destination was. Or even why I was going. And, like it or not, it seemed to be a journey I had to take by myself.

One thing for sure, I would have to get back to the pool tonight. I had to know if she was all right, and warn her about the bear. I slipped in through the back door of the house just as Sandy's alarm sounded.

"Pick up a chicken and some fresh vegetables," Sandy was saying half an hour later. She was composing a verbal shopping list for me. "And French bread, if they've got it." She poked into a cupboard, then the freezer. "And dessert. Ice cream or something." Genny and her father were coming to dinner. Sandy had forgotten to tell me. "Put the chicken in the oven at four."

I jotted down the items, like a waitress. Sandy barely glanced at me. I don't think she would have noticed if I were standing there in a ball gown, or a buckskin dress. A horn honked, and she was out the door. Having logged only thirty minutes in my own bed, I collapsed onto the couch and fell asleep.

. . . Sandy and I are nailing shingles on the roof. We hammer and hammer. But shingles keep coming loose, falling off faster than we can keep up. We are working on opposite sides of the roof. Every time I pound a shingle down, one of Sandy's pops loose. The same happens when Sandy gets one tightened. But we never notice. We just keep hammering, harder and faster. And the house keeps falling apart beneath us . . .

A pounding noise woke me. It was Genny, all freckles and copper-red hair, grinning and pointing at me through the narrow, uncurtained window next to the door. Not much use pretending I wasn't home. I dragged myself to the door.

"Guess what?" she asked, nudging purple-tinted sunglasses up the bridge of her nose as she danced past me into the room. No "*Bonjour*" or anything.

"Good to see you, too. Come on in," I said to the empty porch.

"Who are you talking to?" Genny asked from where she had flopped on the couch.

"Nobody." I pointed to the vacant doorway. "See? Nobody there."

She immediately saw the truth of my words and nodded, apparently satisfied that we had resolved something.

"Guess what?" she said again.

"What?"

"That's not a guess. Come on," she pleaded. She hopped off the couch like popcorn off a hot skillet. "Okay, I'll give you a hint: I heard it on the radio."

"I don't think I'm going to have time to guess."

"Come *on*, Lisa."

"Okay. A volcano erupted out of the springs last night and everybody in town was killed."

"No," she said emphatically. "But you're close."

"I am?"

"Yes. Somebody at the Lodge reported seeing a girl jump in the pool from the balcony last night. You know, that balcony off the second floor?"

"Did they see who it was?" I asked.

"No, that's the spooky part. They couldn't find anyone, or any evidence or anything. But the radio said that the maintenance man found the top rail of the balcony broken a few days ago." I was getting worried, but it must have looked like confusion. "The balcony has that railing. You know," Genny explained, depicting a railing in her own personal sign language.

"I know, I know," I said.

"Why are you sleeping on the couch?" she asked, seeing the pillows and comforter for the first time.

I ignored her question. "So . . . ?" I prompted.

"So what?" Genny asked.

"So go on. About the pool! What else did you hear?"

"Oh. Yeah. Well, the Lodge people think that somebody might have jumped or fallen in that other time, too. So they're going to lock the balcony or post a watchman. Maybe both. They want to protect the guests from sleepwalking accidents or some such thing. That's ridiculous, don't you think? Sleepwalking. I mean, they're not finding dead bodies or anything, are they? I think it's like somebody jumping from the balcony on a dare. Or maybe space alien abductions. Anyway, isn't it exciting? Probably about the most exciting thing this little burg has seen in the last hundred years."

She collapsed on the couch again. Out of gas.

I just nodded weakly. Lock the door to the balcony? My link with the past and the girl would be cut off. Still, somebody saw me. I was lucky not to be caught on the balcony this morning. I had to think this through. But Genny was off and running in another direction.

"What do you say we go swimming and then make the dinner for our parents together?" she suggested. "With candles and flowers. Real special."

Romantic candlelit dinners were not on my priority list, and that Genny could say or even think such a thing disgusted me. But I *was* anxious to get to the Lodge and check out Genny's story. As far as I knew, that balcony was the only way back to my friend.

"Let's go," I agreed.

When we got there the door stood wide open, but a sign on the wall read:

Effective Immediately
THE DOOR TO THE BALCONY
WILL BE LOCKED
10p.m. - 8a.m.
The Management

"They're closing the balcony the same hours the pool's closed so nobody can jump in without getting caught," Genny said.

"Yeah," I said, but Genny read me better than that.

"What's wrong, Lisa? It's not such a big deal. Unless *you're* the night swimmer," she said with a sidelong look. I didn't answer.

We went on into the pool. Although I had little enthusiasm for it at first, the mineral water seemed to lift my spirits as easily as it buoyed my body. While Genny was busy swimming laps and risking her life at the diving board, I rested my head on the lip of the pool and let the water work its magic.

It isn't such a big deal that the door is locked, I decided. After all, how do I know what time I might go back to next? My first two trips, just a few days apart, landed me twelve *years* apart in my friend's world. And though I failed to warn her while I was there, maybe that was for the best, too. Why scare her on the basis of a dream?

In fact, despite the "evidence," I was finding it hard to believe, in the light of day, that any of this could be true in the first place.

Late in the afternoon, limp with relaxation, we walked slowly down Mountain Avenue toward Redpath's. Even Genny seemed subdued and languorous, making small talk about school starting next week, some new clothes she'd bought. Then, across from what appeared to be one of the oldest houses in town, she stopped.

"A witch lives there," she whispered, clenching my forearm.

"A witch?"

"That's what I've heard. All my life, since I was little."

"From whom?"

She shrugged. "Other little kids."

"Well that explains things then, doesn't it? No need to stand here staring." I pushed her along. "How're the Beer brothers?" I asked, more to change the subject than out of genuine interest.

"All I can say is I'm glad we're not having dinner at my house tonight. I haven't got all the feathers picked up yet."

"Are we talking about parakeet plumage here?" I asked.

"No. The brothers just had a disagreement with an old pillow this morning. Lisa, you would not believe how many feathers there are in one pillow. They were everywhere." A laugh exploded out of her.

"So while all this was going on," she continued, "there were Ralph and Abernathy, squashing themselves together on that little stick perch till they looked like Siamese twins, watching feathers drifting by just outside the bars. 'Not us! Not us! We're too young to die. We've got our whole feathered lives ahead of us!'" she squeaked in her best bird voice, pushing against my side and flapping her free arm passionately. "I felt like I was in one of those glass balls. You know, with the village inside, that you shake and turn upside down to get the blizzard?"

We were laughing so hard we walked right past the store and had to go back almost a block.

Inside, I looked in the meat case while Genny picked out salad makings. Someone appeared behind the counter. I glanced up, expecting James or Marie. It was Jay. He wore a butcher's apron and looked as cute as I remembered.

"Hi," he said.

"Hi." I gulped a mouthful of saliva, making a noise that could be heard across the street. "Do you work here?"

It wasn't a great recovery, but did Genny have to stare at me like I'd just called myself by the wrong name or something? Big help. Very big help.

"No," Jay said. "I just like to stand behind the counter wearing an apron. I do it in all the stores."

I was speechless.

"It's a joke," Jay said. "I'm joking. Yes, I work here. Actually, I live here, eat here, sleep here, and work here." His eyes sparkled blue and his hair gleamed black. "It's my parents' store."

I thought I was going to tell him about how I'd been looking for him but all that came out was, "Sorry about the library."

"Yeah, I wondered what happened."

"I hope you didn't wait too long or anything."

He shook his head. "No big deal. I got into some reading and kind of forgot everything else. As usual."

"You, too? I do the same thing. My mother's ready to kill me sometimes." I rattled on with a few too many examples of when and why, reminding myself of Genny.

"Well, anyway, what happened is that Sandy — that's my mother — she kind of needed me, I guess. We moved into our new house that day. Our old new house. It's right down Mountain. So. I really am sorry."

"It's okay. No problem."

There was an awkward silence. I wanted to set up another time at the library, but I was afraid to ask.

"Did you want something?" he asked. For a startled moment I thought he had read my mind. But he was pointing to the meat case.

"Oh. Yeah. A chicken, please. That one." He placed the plastic-bagged chicken on the counter a moment later and, as I reached for it, my fingers brushed his hand. I jerked back. "I'm sorry," I said, as if I had damaged his hand.

"Would you like to take a hike?" He laughed. "That didn't come out right. I mean, *go* on a hike with me? Sunday, maybe?"

"A hike? Sure," I said. Hiking was not one of my favorite things. In fact, I'd never been on a hike, unless I counted the ninth grade field trip to the St. Louis Art Museum. But being with Jay would make up for it, I hoped.

"I'll pick you up at eleven and provide the lunch, too. We can spend the whole afternoon. I know a great spot."

By some miracle I thought to tell him my address and turned to leave, feeling pretty pleased with the way things had worked out. Was I up to a whole afternoon of hiking, though? I hoped so. I didn't want to let him down again.

I was practically out on the sidewalk when I heard an ear-splitting whistle from behind me. I turned, and there was Genny, slouched up against the checkout counter, looking like she owned the place. Carrots, lettuce, spinach, and tomatoes waited on the counter behind her. My poor deserted chicken swung from her hand like a lumpy pendulum. She was grinning so hard I thought her freckles would break.

9

"You look wonderful tonight."

"So do you."

"You've done a great job decorating."

"How sweet of you to notice, John."

Sandy and Genny's father were forming a mutual admiration society right at the dinner table. But when the compliments gushed over to include, "Aren't these kids great!" and, "What a meal they put together!" Genny and I just looked at each other and got out of there as fast as we could.

She took me to The Mountaineer Shop so I could buy a pair of hiking boots for "your date" as Genny liked to describe it. I was glad to get away from the house but two hours later, my arms full of shoes, a jacket, flannel shirt, cotton-blend pants, a half dozen pairs of socks and a heavy duty nylon daypack, I was afraid to go back. Genny pronounced me an official Coloradan.

"Yeah, well, when Sandy sees the charge at the end of the month I'm going to be an official *dead* Coloradan."

"Gee, in that case maybe I should let your mom know that you and I wear the same size boots."

At eleven sharp on Sunday Jay rumbled up our gravel drive in an old Datsun station wagon. He leaped the porch steps with a single stride. Hoping for a quick getaway, I opened the door before he had a chance to knock.

"Wow, you look like a real professional," he said, eyeing my new hiking boots and sturdy pants. I'd been worrying about overdoing it and now I was sure I had. He was wearing jeans, old running shoes and a blue, combed-cotton shirt that almost matched his eyes.

"Yeah, well, we'll see." I lifted my foot, cradling my ankle to display the unscuffed sole to Jay. "I just hope these things work as well outside as they did on the shoe store carpet," I said. Jay smiled.

"Better bring a jacket or something," he said. "The weather can change in a minute around here." The sky was cloudless and didn't give a hint of anything other to come, but I grabbed the jacket.

"What are we doing? Climbing Kilimanjaro?"

Sandy drifted in from the kitchen. "Are you leaving?" she asked innocently, as if she didn't know about my plans for the day. Wondering if her ploy to meet Jay was as obvious to him as it was to me, I opened the door full wide and stepped back out of the way.

"Sandy, this is Jay Redpath. Jay, my mother, Sandy Carey."

Before Jay could say hello or goodbye Sandy said, "Your parents are James and Marie from down at the store, I understand."

"That's right, Mrs. Carey."

"Please, call me Sandy," she said.

"Okay. Sandy," he said, extending his hand. Before their hands separated, Sandy was telling him how friendly his parents are and how happy she is to be in Indian Springs. While Jay listened politely to her rundown of her first week at work, I stepped outside and slowly pulled the door shut between them.

"'Bye, Sandy! See you later!" I said with false friendliness as I snugged the door against the stop and heard the satisfying *click* of the latch. "Sorry about that," I said to Jay. "She doesn't know when to quit."

He looked at me. "You were disrespectful," he said.

"Yeah, well it was either that or bring her with us," I said, my tone full of excuse.

Jay reached past me and opened the door again. Sandy wasn't there. "Nice meeting you, Mrs. . . . . Sandy," he said quietly, then closed the door again gently. He didn't say anything more about it, but it seemed like a long trip from the door to the car.

While Jay tossed my pack and jacket into the back, I opened the rust-spattered passenger door and plopped onto shredded foam rubber and flaps of brittle vinyl that passed for a passenger seat. Jay slid behind the wheel and inserted a key into the ignition cylinder, which dangled precariously beneath the dash, supported only by taped electrical wires. A glare from a crack which meandered across the windshield stabbed at my eyes. Jay snapped his seat belt in place and instructed me to do the same.

"Why? Does this thing run or something?" I teased.

He grabbed the ignition switch with one hand and held it firm as he turned the key with the other. The engine caught instantly and settled down to a barely audible hum. "Like a top," he said with satisfaction. I snapped my belt in place.

The sun was high in the sky as we drove into the hills. After a while the paved road gave way to gravel and the distant snow-covered peaks were swallowed up one after another by smaller, closer hills. A few more miles and we turned off onto another, narrower gravel road bordered by aspen. A car eased past and the driver waved. Jay waved back.

"Who's that?" I asked.

"I don't know."

"Why'd you wave, then?"

He shrugged. "People just wave, whether they know each other or not."

As if to prove it another car went by, the man and woman inside waving at us like old friends.

"People seem friendlier out here," I said waving at a family picnicking along the roadside as if I'd known them all my life. They all waved back. Even the baby.

"They can afford to be. They're not bumping into each other all the time."

Where I came from people were always pushing past each other, rushing to get where they wanted to go. You couldn't possibly say hello to everyone so I guess it was easier to ignore everybody instead. I was used to that kind of anonymity. I'd always thought I liked it.

"And it's not just that," Jay said. "There's a sense of needing each other out here. I think it happens whenever

74

people get enough space between themselves and the next person. It helps you feel the connections again."

We jolted down the road past several small gem-like lakes, their cobalt blue a reflection of the cloudless sky. Just past an expanse of grassy meadow, Jay turned onto a yet narrower road — two matted strips of grass, really — which plunged headlong into the trees.

"Now we're in national forest," he said. His eyes shone as if he'd just returned home after a long absence. A little further on, the road ended in a turnabout. He pulled over, almost nudging a lichen-splashed boulder that was bigger than the car, and turned off the engine.

We got our stuff from the back and started out. Jay had parked in a small peninsula of trees and we were soon at sea in the rolling meadow, flanked on all sides by a shoreline of stately ponderosa pines. Birds too blue to be real *chirrupp*ed gaily, suspended themselves in mid air like feathered helicopters, then made effortless, impossible landings on the tips of tall meadow flowers and stood like statues.

"Mountain bluebirds," Jay announced. He bent to pluck a small orange-red flower and gave it to me. "Sulphurflower. It means fall is coming soon. Not many wildflowers left now, but next spring there'll be dozens of varieties. We'll have to come back then." For the first time since my arrival in Colorado I didn't feel like going back to St. Louis quite so fast.

We entered the pine forest, crunching over a thick mat of dried needles underfoot. The aroma was heady, stronger than any so-called air freshener and definitely more pleasant. Low green bushes blanketed the space under many of the trees.

"What are those?" I asked.

"Kinnikinnik."

"Kinnikinnik," I said, savoring the sound as it clicked past my teeth.

"Very important plant to the Utes. The leaves were dried and smoked in pipes. It has edible fruit, too," he said, bending to pluck a few tiny red berries from the ground-hugging plant. "Want some?"

"Uh, I don't think so," I said, and Jay popped the little nuggets into his mouth. Something large and heavy *whooshed* overhead. I ducked instinctively.

"It's all right," Jay whispered, taking my hands off my head and holding them in his own. He was standing behind me. I felt him bend a little. He's going to kiss me, I thought. But I was wrong. Maybe I was disappointed.

"It's an owl," Jay said. He was still whispering. "Kind of unusual to see one in the middle of the day." He let go of one of my hands and pointed. I looked just in time to see a blimp-like bird disappear into dense upper branches.

"Why are we whispering?" I whispered. Jay laughed, and let go of my other hand.

"I don't know. Owls are special."

"Where did it come from?" I said. "I didn't even hear it until it was on top of me."

"Neither do the mice or rabbits," Jay answered.

"Aw, poor things."

"Hey, I didn't hear you crying over that chicken I handed you a few days ago." He looked at me. "Same

76

difference," he said. "Only I respect the owl's approach more," he added.

We walked hand in hand through the tall trees in silence for a while. "There's a legend among many Native American tribes about the owl," Jay said. "When an Old One hears the owl call her name, she knows she will soon pass on to the Afterlife."

"Do you believe that?" I asked.

"A few days before she died, my grandmother told me she heard the owl call her name. She didn't mean a real, physical owl. She heard the owl call her name in here," he said, lightly touching his chest. "She knew her circle on the earth was closing."

"She really knew she was going to die?"

"The Old Ones say that those who live in harmony with the cycles of nature are in touch with their own natural cycle, too."

We came out of the pines to a clearing surrounding a small pond. A stiff breeze pushed tiny white-capped waves across its surface.

"My father died eight months ago," I said, surprising myself.

"I know," Jay said, and pressed my hand into his. It felt good.

As we clambered up onto a huge flat slab of granite next to the pond there was a commotion at the far side of the water. Six ducks, which I had not seen earlier, fairly ran across the wave tops before breaking free of the surface and circling sharply away from us.

"See this?" Jay fingered the branches and leaves of a small, woody bush next to our rock. "Wild rose," he said. It did look like a miniature version of a rose bush, prickly stems and all, but no blossom. "It's past flowering and the rosehips are just beginning to swell. Look." He rubbed several tiny nodules hanging from the branches. "They'll be bigger and red-ripe in a month or so. Good food for the winter."

Jay took a bag, a bowl, and two cups out of his pack. He poured a pale orange-colored powder from the bag into the bowl, added some water from his canteen, and stirred. A spicy aroma rose immediately, blending tantalizingly with the smell of sage from plants which sprouted in a sunny spot just behind our rock.

"What's that?" I said.

"Hummus," Jay said, tilting the creamy mixture toward me. Images of manure, grass clippings, and rotted melon rinds brought me up short.

"You mean like what they put on gardens and crops?" I asked, trying to hide my alarm.

"Not humus," he laughed. "Hummus. Garbanzo beans, tahini, lemon and spices."

"Oh. Yeah," I said as nonchalantly as I could manage. "Hummus. My father and I had some once at a Middle Eastern restaurant. It was good."

"Well, this isn't exactly gourmet," he said, "but it's tasty. And nice and light for backpacking. Anyway, this won't be as good as you had since we don't have any olive oil to drizzle over it."

But it did taste as good. We dipped it with corn chips and crunched sweet carrots in between, and there in the sage-filled air with the sun shining on the water, it was every bit as good. We followed it with apples that snapped like miniature firecrackers with every bite.

"Ready for a little rock climbing?" Jay asked as we stashed our trash in the pack.

"I don't think so," I said, looking a quarter-mile beyond the pond at a wall of vertical rock shooting up two or three hundred feet above the valley.

"Not those," he said. He took hold of my shoulders and gently turned me toward a manageable looking mound of granite boulders. "These."

The climb proved to be challenge enough. Boulders were stacked on boulders and they were all covered with lichen of many colors — black, red, grey, orange, and a green that was neon-bright — as though cans of paint had been thrown against them. He led the way, pointing out footholds, warning me to "keep an eye out for rattlers," and offering a welcome hand up once in a while. When we reached the top a spasmodic wind shoved me first one direction and then the other, trying to blow me off like an invisible king-of-the-hill challenger. I sat down fast.

"How do you know this thing won't roll or something?" I asked, hoping Jay wouldn't hear the catch in my voice. "You know, because of our extra weight, I mean."

"I don't."

"Oh! Great!" I yelled against a sudden burst of wind. "Just what I wanted to hear!"

"But since this rock probably tips the scale at about fifty tons, I figure our weight doesn't matter too much." He shrugged his shoulders, then gestured broadly toward the horizon. "What a view, huh?"

It was good I was still sitting down because the view took my breath away. Snow-topped peaks, many of them over fourteen thousand feet high Jay told me, cut a jagged horizon far to the east. In front of these were lesser but still impressive ranges which stood one in front of the other, like waves on an angry, frozen sea. Closest to us, hills wrapped in green sloped down to the wildflower-dotted meadow below our rocky tower.

I lay down on my stomach, feeling the sun-warmed rock beneath me, and propped my chin with my forearm. Jay pointed out a path that wound down to where two trickles of water joined to form a larger stream.

"My ancestors used that way to the water," he said.

"Does the stream have a name?"

"The maps list it as Bull Creek. Grandmother said Nuu-chi called it Singing Waters. Listen."

The water gurgled and splashed over the rocks as it flowed down through the valley.

"'The water sings in celebration of life,' my grandmother told me. 'The journey of Singing Waters is one of change and movement. It parallels the life of our tribe. From the highlands in the summer, to the valleys in winter. As long as the water flows it sings. The People, also.'"

Our eyes met for a moment, but it was too intense. I looked away.

I watched light and shadow play tag on the ponderosa pine that covered the hills across the stream. I thought I knew why the Utes called these the Shining Mountains — every single pine needle gleamed, and the snow on the distant peaks sparkled.

A quiet settled gently over me. I began to notice that I felt different somehow. My mind was curiously empty. I had a feeling of being more than alive and my senses seemed super-alert. Yet I was perfectly comfortable. The stone beneath me had become a cloud, and I a part of it. When I felt my body at all, I felt larger than normal, yet lighter. The notion crossed my mind that I might be glowing. For a few magical moments I had the sense of being astonishingly beautiful. And that I was part of something larger, and more beautiful still.

Jay's shoes scuffed the rock and it became real beneath me once more. He stretched out next to me.

"I call this Meditation Rock," he said. "I look at the clouds, clear my mind, and listen for an answer. Dreaming doesn't work for me."

"Dreaming?"

"Some people can see the future in their dreams, or get answers to questions. Others get questions to answer," he said. "At least they used to. The Dreaming Ones were the shamans, the medicine men and women. Anyway, if my dreams are telling me things, I haven't been able to read them. But up here, answers sometimes come."

I was intrigued. "Like about what?"

"Like what to do next. Like go to the University of Colorado or stay here and work in the store, maybe attend community college . . ." His voice trailed off. He sat up straight and looked at me. "My father wants me to go, before it's too late."

I remembered the words I'd heard in the store that first day. "Too late for what?" I asked.

"I don't know. To find myself, he says. I think he means to make something of myself. He's worried I'll end up like a lot of his mother's people. Like his uncle, for example.

"What happened to him?" I asked.

"He was taken."

"What do you mean? Kidnapped?"

"That's not what they called it, but that's about right. He was taken by the Bureau of Indian Affairs people, put in a boarding school. It happened all the time. Grandmother told me that in the school the kids weren't allowed to practice their Ute ways. They couldn't speak Ute. They couldn't wear Ute clothes. Their long hair was cut short. They were taught to be like whites in every way."

"What did he do?"

Jay shrugged. "Just what you'd expect, I guess. The traditions and values that meant everything to him — anything Ute — were unacceptable to the culture he was forced to live in. He was told, over and over, that Ute meant heathen, uncivilized, inferior." He picked distractedly at something golden on the rock surface. "He was only a little boy," he said. "He gave up his Ute ways. He tried to be white."

Jay was quiet for a few moments. Then he let out a sigh. "It didn't work, though. He was caught in the middle. No matter what he did, he still wasn't good enough. The whites looked down on him. He started drinking when he was fourteen. By the time he was twenty, I guess it was pretty heavy stuff. He spent most of the rest of his life drinking or drunk. He died of alcoholism when he was fifty-one. I never knew him."

I turned on my side to look at Jay just as he jumped to his feet in one smooth feline move and looked off into the hills, oblivious to the sheer drop a few feet away.

"But with Grandmother things were different. Her parents hid her when the BIA people came. She never went to school. As I was growing up, she was always there for me. I could have learned more from her. I should have, too, but I thought I had better things to do."

He shook his head angrily. Then he sat crosslegged in front of me, hands on his knees, his eyes glowing. "I remember something else she told me," he said. I sat up and turned toward him.

"She said that the Nuu-ci — the People, the Utes — have wisdom. We see far and live in harmony and appreciation of our Mother Earth. We have heart knowledge.

"The Marika-ci — the white people — she said that they are full of mind knowledge. She told me that they know little things — facts, I think she meant — that they see close and can make anything. 'This gives them great power,' she said, 'which they do not know how to use because they are blind beyond where they stand. And they have closed their hearts.

"'One day,' my grandmother said, 'the Nuu-ci and the Marika-ci will flow together, just as the streams from opposite sides of the valley merge below to make the great river.' She said that they will learn from each other and enrich each other's spirits, and that there will be born then a new people, far-seeing and with great power, full of wisdom and strength."

It was several moments before I could speak.

"That's beautiful," I said. "She sounds like she was a wonderful person." Without thinking, I reached out and took his hands in mine. Our knees were almost touching. My breathing speeded up and we sat that way for a time before a pressure in his grip told me he was about to speak again.

"I wouldn't be happy working in the store, owning it some day, spending my life there. My father and mother seem happy enough with that, but I know it's not right for me. They know it, too. That's why my father wants me to go to college. He wants me to be "successful," like his brother. He's an engineer at some big firm in Boulder. Uncle Bill is the good example they want me to follow. He's offered to let me live at his house so I can attend the university there. He's even willing to help with tuition." More hand pressure. "So. That's what I'm going to do. Go to Boulder at the end of the week and try to late-register."

His words struck me like lightning from the blue: He was leaving. I was just getting to know him, to like him, and he was leaving. I turned my head and swallowed hard, then coughed as the muscles in my throat knotted. I jerked my hands away from Jay's to wipe my face, embarrassed.

"Are you okay?" he asked.

"Sure," I said. "Just a crumb of food or something." I smiled and hoped it passed for the real thing.

On the way back to the car, as we neared the tree line where the forest opened onto the meadow, Jay suddenly stopped. Several steps behind him, I stopped, too, maintaining the protective barrier I had placed between us. I was startled by the perfect stillness, like at a symphony at that moment when the conductor raises his baton just before the opening note.

"Lisa, I'm going to miss you, too, you know," Jay said, still facing the empty forest in front of him.

I was vaguely aware of a dull, far-off drone, punctuated by the snap of pine needles under his feet as Jay turned to face me.

"I . . . like you," he said. He reached out his hand. We just stood there, living sculptures for a few moments. I took his outstretched hand, still a little uncertain.

I heard the droning again. It swelled quickly, like the roar of a fast-approaching train.

"What's that noise?" I said as the sound rushed toward us. Before Jay could answer, a blast of freezing wind pounded my back, pushing me against him in an unintended hug. Another gust hit now, even more violent. Trees swayed and groaned. The whole sky was heavy with black clouds and thunder rumbled all around. Missouri memories lunged into consciousness. A tornado was upon us!

"Come on! Let's run for it!" Jay shouted, pulling me by my hand just as instinct told me we should throw ourselves to the ground.

"It's a tornado!" I said.

"No, it's not! Run fast!" he shouted.

"I'm scared," I shouted back.

"Run anyway!"

Gigantic droplets of water pelted us as we dashed out into the open meadow toward the car a hundred endless yards beyond. Just before we reached it hailstones, some as big as marbles, bombarded us. We dove into the car, nearly cracking heads, and laughed with the sudden relief of being able to watch the weather through glass.

"This is why you always bring bad-weather gear into the mountains," Jay said. He didn't seem to notice that I was drenched through.

"Couldn't have done without it," I said, dramatically yanking my dry jacket out of my pack and holding it up for him to see.

"Yep, good thing I told you to bring that," he said.

"Absolutely."

It wasn't a tornado, but it was the fiercest, most sudden thunderstorm I had ever been in. And it was getting worse. The hail intensified, golf ball size stones slapping the glass and sliding down into a growing heap at the bottom of the windshield. I didn't feel quite so safe behind the thin glass anymore.

"But it's still summer," I shouted over the din on the roof.

"Doesn't matter," Jay shouted back. "The temperature can nosedive in a matter of minutes in the mountains. You can have snow in July!" I believed him.

The hail stopped as suddenly as it had begun and, miraculously, by the time we had dried ourselves as best we could, the sun was shining low above the western horizon. Jay started up the car and we sloshed our way through ruts and puddles. We sang old songs all the way home. Before we were halfway there the sky was cloudless again and a giant ghostly moon loomed above the eastern horizon.

"Let's do something together tomorrow," Jay said when we pulled up to my house. The moon had brightened. He took my hand. "Go swimming maybe."

"Okay," I said, happy at the thought, yet feeling a kind of inner tearing because he was leaving in just a few days.

He walked with me to the door. Through the front window I could see into the dimly lit living room. Sandy and Mr. Smith were sitting close together on the couch. Light from the TV flickered across them. I watched Sandy lean forward and scoop up a big handful of popcorn from a bowl on the table. She turned toward John Smith. Her lips moved. He smiled. Sandy dropped nuggets of popcorn into his cupped hands. I turned away from the glass.

Jay was close behind me, so close I almost hit him as I spun.

"Jay, —"

The word slipped out quickly, a reflex, before his eyes caught mine. His hands touched me just above my elbows, then slid slowly up toward my shoulders. He leaned forward, ducking a little and tilting his head, and kissed me lightly on the lips.

Moments later his car was backing down our driveway. I stood there on the porch, and watched that old Datsun slip smoothly out of sight before I went in.

10

The next evening, sitting together in the steaming waters of the hot pool, Jay massaged my shoulders while he planned aloud his busy schedule of packing and saying goodbye over the next few days to everyone in his large extended family. Once, there was a long silence, when I was supposed to talk, I guess. I didn't know what I felt, much less what to say, so I didn't say anything. Jay kissed me on the back of the head. He said that he would be back at Thanksgiving. It was the last time I saw him before he left.

A letter came the next week, telling me about his uncle's large house, and all the excitement of being on the Boulder campus. I wrote a short letter back, still not really knowing what to say, wishing him happiness, although he sounded plenty happy already.

John Smith showed up the next day, tool box in hand, and helped Sandy put up the porch swing she'd wanted. Almost every evening after that they sat there talking — sometimes for hours, close and quiet.

It was nice having him around in some ways. It took Sandy's attention off running my life. And he was a good listener. Not only for Sandy, but for me and Genny, too. But just by being there he reminded me that my father wasn't. I couldn't blame him for that, but it hurt just the same. And, fair or not, I held it against him.

Worries about the adopted Ute girl gnawed at me almost every day. I couldn't shake a feeling of responsibility. A need to help her somehow. But the balcony door remained locked tight.

To my surprise, I was relieved when school started. Textbooks and teachers and homework seemed like safe, familiar territory compared to the mine field I'd been walking.

Genny and I walked the six blocks to school together that first day. As was our usual arrangement, Genny talked, I listened. She'd been awake practically all night, she said. Too excited to sleep, she said. I was absolutely going to love Springs High, she said.

"Genny, you've never gone to Springs High."

"So?"

"So how do you know I'm going to love it? How do you know *either* of us is going to love it?"

"I don't follow you. Why wouldn't we?"

After the last class Genny met me at my locker, her arms linked with those of two boys.

"Lisa," she said, her eyes flashing, "isn't that teacher gorgeous?" The boys rolled their eyes in disdain.

I scanned the teacherless hallway. "What teacher, Genny?"

"You know. Biology. Mister . . . what's his name?"

"Burrows?" I offered.

"Burrows. That's it, yeah. I mean, he is definitely biological."

90

One of the boys, the dark-haired one, cleared his throat. Twice.

"Oh, where are my manners?" Genny pretended to scold herself. "Lisa, this is Chris." She stabbed him in the ribs with her elbow. He winced, then smiled. "And this is Michael. You remember, I told you about him." She grinned up at the exceptionally tall redhead on her right.

"Hi, Chris," I said. "Hi, Michael."

"We're all in Biology together," Michael said. I think he was talking to me. He was looking at Genny.

"Michael helped me get my menagerie together. Then he deserted me," Genny said, flinging her arm across her forehead and falling backward dramatically. Luckily, Michael caught her before she hit the ground.

"I was on vacation in August," Michael corrected as he tipped Genny upright. "With my family. We went to the coast. San Diego."

"I've been there," Genny said. "I think."

We walked out the school doors and up Olive toward Mountain Avenue. Michael slipped his hands into his pockets. Freckles dotted his wrist and mingled with the red-blond hair on his forearm.

"You two look enough alike to be brother and sister," I said.

Genny's and Michael's eyebrows went up as though pulled by a puppeteer's string.

"That's what Genny's always worrying about," Michael said.

"That you look like brother and sister?"

"No, that we might *be* brother and sister," he said.

91

"He's just about convinced me we're not," Genny said.

"Why would you think that he's your brother?" I asked Genny.

She got a sudden sick look on her face. "You never know," she mumbled.

Something told me it was time to change the subject, but Genny did it for me. "Hey, Chris," she said. "Where were you all summer?"

"St. Louis. I've got an aunt and uncle and some cousins there."

"Lisa, you're from St. Louis!" Genny exclaimed.

"I know," I reminded her.

"Hot place," Chris said. I nodded. "It's a lot nicer here. The weather, I mean. But my cousins are fun. I go there every summer."

"Did you guys ever think, maybe you already know each other?" Genny said. She met my question-mark face with her version of a rational answer. "You know, because you lived there and Chris goes there every year."

"Maybe they're brother and sister," Michael said.

"I don't think we know each other," Chris said. "There's about a million people in St. Louis."

"St. Louis is not Indian Springs," I said, as though populousness were next to godliness.

"There's a lot of stuff to see and do there," Chris said.

"Yes, there is," I agreed.

"Hey, why don't we all go see a movie on Friday?" Chris said.

"See," Genny said to me, "we have things to do here, too."

"At the Crest?" Michael asked, alarm in his voice.

"Where else?" Genny said.

"Lisa, it's real cool," Chris said. "The seats try to slide you off."

"Sounds like a real treat," I said.

"Okay," Chris said as we reached the intersection of Olive and Mountain. "See you Friday then."

"Aren't you coming to school the rest of the week?" Genny asked.

"Oh. Yeah," Chris said. "I forgot."

"Chris and I live up this way," Michael explained. He pointed further up Olive.

"Michael has to walk Chris home so he doesn't get lost," Genny said in a stage whisper.

"Hey, see that?" Chris said to me, ignoring Genny. "That's Old Lady MacGregor's house." He pointed down Mountain toward the house Genny had told me about earlier.

"What's the story on her anyway?" Genny asked. "I've been hearing about her since I was a little kid."

"What have you heard?" Chris asked.

"You know, that she's real mean, a witch. Stuff like that."

"Well, see? That's the story." Chris grinned.

"I heard she's lived here since the town was founded," Michael said.

"She looks old enough, anyway," Chris said. Then he put on a pretty good Dracula voice, trilling his r's and bouncing his eyebrows: "There is a legend in these mountains . . . that children . . . very, very, *very* small

93

children" — he lowered his hand down, down, down, stopping inches above the ground — "are lured into the old woman's house . . . and never . . . ever . . . seen again."

"You're teasing," I said.

"What is 'tease'?" Dracula replied. "I just tell you the legend."

"Cute, *mais non*?" Genny said after we'd gotten out of earshot up Mountain.

"You and Michael *could* be brother and sister, though."

"Quit it." Genny grabbed my arm and twirled me around. "You know what I would really like?" She looked me right in the eyes. "For you and me to be sisters. What do you say?"

"I would say that I believe that was settled about sixteen years back," I said. "Anyway, I don't think it could work."

"Why not?" she asked with a frown.

"I don't have freckles *or* red hair." I thought it was pretty funny, but Genny didn't. She was serious.

"Well, I was wishing I had a sister," I started, thinking of the little girl on the ledge, and before I knew what hit me Genny had me in a bear hug. "Ow!" I yelled. "Okay, okay. You don't have to get rough about it." She eased up enough that I could breathe again. "So we'll be sisters," I said. She squeezed again, like a vise.

"Do you think your mom likes my dad?" she asked in a trying-to-be-nonchalant voice as we walked toward her house.

I shot her a look. "Don't, Genny," I said, suddenly fierce. "Don't even think about it."

Genny studied me for a moment.

"Okay," she said. "I'll quit while I'm ahead. For now."

The week sped by. Biology with Mr. Burrows was a real surprise. He was not only "biological" as Genny had said, he was a dynamite teacher. Genny, Michael, Chris, and I walked home together every day.

Genny had decided to make dinner that Friday night for our two families, before the movie. I promised I would help her with the meal, but only after she promised to lay off the stuff about her dad and Sandy. Friday after school she wanted me to come straight to her house, but I told her I had something to do at home first. Which was true, although I don't think she would have understood, because what I had to do was be alone for awhile. That's one of the biggest differences between Genny and me: I need more alone time than she does.

I sat at the window seat, gazing out at the meadow far below and remembered my friend from the past. Was she living somewhere there in the meadow, existing in her time as real as I exist in mine? What was she doing? Was it winter or summer? Was she alive or dead? I'd checked the balcony three times since Jay left. Always locked. But tourist season was over now. Things change. Maybe I should try again. I would be risking discovery by Sandy, though, and if she caught me sneaking out of the house at night she'd never let me out of her sight again.

I looked at the clock. Almost five. I was supposed to be at Genny's at five, but I didn't want to go just now. The girl from the past and her people didn't use clocks. They didn't have to plan events for a certain minute. They didn't have calendars either, I suppose. At least not like we have. And were they any the worse off for it? Clocks and calendars run our lives, controlling and limiting us days, weeks, even years in advance. Demanding that we get up, go to bed, eat dinner. Telling us when to work or play. The library, the Lodge, school, — everything in town opens and closes its doors on the dictates of the clock and calendar.

Without them, I realized, life would be more connected to internal rhythms and external realities. I'd eat when I was hungry, or when there was food to be had, not when it was *time* to eat. I would mark time by the sun and the moon.

And the seasons. What if I couldn't depend on heating and cooling systems and light at the flick of a switch, all these things that cut me off from the seasons and the weather? Sure, they're comfortable and convenient, but what am I missing as a result? Maybe the kind of atunement to nature that Jay's grandmother had, talking owls and singing waters. Maybe special wisdom about the cycles of life. Wisdom that might make our conveniences mean something. Maybe a healthy planet. Healthy people. Maybe peaceful dreams.

I remembered what Jay's grandmother said about the Nuu-ci and the Marika-ci: wisdom and strength. And the feeling I had when Jay and I were on the rocks overlooking the place where the two streams joined.

I looked at the clock. Time to go.

96

Dinner went okay, until the end. Sandy was telling John about some books of my father's that she thought he'd like.

"Dad's books!" I blurted. "You're giving Dad's books away? You can't do that!"

My mother stared as if she'd never seen me before, and for a moment it looked as if even Genny was reconsidering the advantages of being an only child.

"Lisa, they're books," Sandy said. "Your dad would want them to be read."

"Didn't you even think that *I* might want them?"

I jumped out of my seat and ran out of the room. Out of the house. It wasn't until I reached my own front door that I discovered I was still clutching my fork.

A gentle tap on my bedroom door woke me. I was sprawled on the bed, fully clothed.

"Lisa, it's me."

I sat up. Realized it was Genny.

"Oh. Come on in."

Genny came in, but she wasn't wearing her usual grin. The whole terrible scene at the dinner table flooded in.

"Chris and Michael are at my house," she said. "You're going, aren't you?"

"I don't know. Going where?"

"To the movie, you nitwit!"

"Thanks a lot," I snapped.

In one quick move Genny was on the bed next to me. "You're not a nitwit," she said. "I am. I'm the nitwit. Sometimes I don't think before I talk. I'm sorry." She brushed a clump of scraggly hair from my cheek. "And your mother's really sorry, too. She said she was wrong not to ask you about the books first."

I didn't say anything.

"Come on, Lisa, don't let this stop our plans. It's Friday. They're waiting for us. They're hunks. Biological hunks."

Although I thought I was in no mood for it, I laughed. I scooted off the bed and studied my tear-streaked face and frazzled hair in the mirror. Genny was right. Why let my anger at Sandy run my life? Whether she was at fault or not, why punish myself?

"Give me a minute," I said to Genny's reflection in the glass.

"All *right*," Genny said.

Despite my good intentions, my mood returned and persisted through the high-tech-futuristic-action-hero movie. Watching the others clown around in the pizza place afterwards, though, I saw that I was letting my anger — at Sandy, or somebody — control me again. I realized how much I liked these guys. And that it was Genny who had drawn me out so easily with her carefree, gregarious way that I had hardly felt it happening. I could choose to have a good time.

It took a conscious decision, an effort, but I finally let myself have fun. I went to bed at midnight, tired and happy.

. . . A huge, faceless, man-machine, sweat-greased muscles crisscrossed with bulging veins, points a machine gun menacingly at a group of people. They have thick, black hair, the men's in braids, the women's loose. Their skin is dark and they all wear buckskin. A blond, fair-skinned girl sits among them. The cyborg's finger flexes, and the gun erupts in a long, fevered burst. The people fall without a cry, like actors in a silent movie.

Except for the little girl. She screams and clings to the bodies littering the ground. She screams again when she sees the red on her hands, and smears it into her yellow hair. She runs then, still screaming, into the arms of my father. The gun blasts again and they, too, fall dead to the ground . . .

My father sits at the crest of a lush green hill, alive and well. The old Indian lady, Leaves Always Green, is with him. I'm in the dream now, too. A rugged valley separates us. My father sees me. He smiles. He waves. I wave back, happy . . .

I woke with a start. But I wasn't screaming. I wasn't crying. Those days were past.

I slipped out into the dark and headed straight to the Lodge.

11

The door to the balcony wasn't locked. The sign had been taken down. I closed the door behind me, and hoped no one had seen me.

I whispered "Spirit" as I had the other times. The water girl appeared. Without a thought I jumped in. Our hands touched. A century fell away and I found myself on the shore of the natural pool. The air was warm. The bushes and trees were in full leaf. Summer.

My friend was alive and sitting nearby at the edge of the pool. Leaves Always Green was beside her. No one else was in sight. The reddish-skinned teepees up the river were strangely silent. Not a horse or a human moved anywhere. It was like a painting, just a painting of an old west scene.

Except for my friend and the old woman. They were talking intently. The girl looked my way, nodded once. A greeting. Except for the change in season it was as if no time had passed since our last meeting. Had I arrived before or after the Bear Dance? Had she survived or did I still need to warn her? I couldn't tell.

I sat on a rock a few feet from the two women. Leaves Always Green glanced in my direction with just a trace of a smile. Could she see me, too? Was she pretending not to?

Suddenly I heard a rumble, and felt it, too, through the ground. It grew louder and louder, until it was thunder. Twenty horsemen rode out of the hills then, their faces painted yellow and black. Long braids bounced on their shoulders and some held weapons raised high in the air. They headed straight for us. Leaves Always Green and her granddaughter rose and faced them.

What are they doing, I wondered? Don't they see the danger?

"Run! Run!" I screamed, but they stood their ground.

Clouds of dust burst like smoke from the horses' hooves and the ground shook beneath my feet. I wanted to grab the two women, make them run to safety, but it was already too late. The horses and their menacing riders were upon us. I stumbled back, threw myself headlong to one side.

I lay there, paralyzed by my fear, unable even to throw my arm across my face. An instant before the slaughter, Leaves Always Green raised a hand, as if to greet the attackers. To my amazement, the apparent leader of the group raised his hand in similar fashion, and the entire band came to a sudden halt only yards in front of us.

I know this man, I thought, as I watched him throw his leg effortlessly over his horse's neck and leap lithely to the ground. Another wave of fear rushed over me as he snatched the girl up into his arms, but I saw the smile on her face as the big man spun with her and set her back down on her feet.

I remembered him now. He was the man she had selected for marriage at the Bear Dance. But had I come now before that time or after? Was she safe, or must I still warn her?

"We will stop them," he said to the two women. "Never again will they come to take our healing waters."

"Colorow is a great leader," said Leaves Always Green.

"The other women and the children have gone to Singing Waters for safety. You must go, too," Colorow said.

"Colorow," my friend objected, "I wish to stay here and wait for your return."

"You are my wife," Colorow said.

She had survived!

Then Leaves Always Green spoke, with calm authority. "You will return victorious," she said. She turned back to the pool. "We will wait."

Colorow did not argue. He touched his fingertips to his wife's, then jumped in one fluid motion onto the high back of his brown and white horse. Colorow and his warriors turned and rode swiftly down the valley, into the trees and out of sight, as though they were one being, guided by a single mind.

My friend clutched the arm of the smaller woman. "Will he return, or will our enemies come, Grandmother?"

"You have ears that hear," she said with a teasing smile. "My dreaming tells me he will be triumphant, this time." The young woman loosened her grip on her grandmother's arm, but her eyes remained sad. "What have you dreamed, my daughter?" the old woman asked.

102

My friend eased her grandmother onto the grassy bank beside the warm pool, then knelt alongside her and sat back on her heels. "I dreamed it was summer," she began, "full, ripe, and green. The People lived well and free. Then clouds covered our sky, dark and heavy and filled with fire. It was a great and powerful storm, like no other the People have ever known. It came from the east where storms do not live. The winds of this storm were fierce and blew all creatures before it to where the sun sets. After . . ."

She sighed deeply. Leaves Always Green laid her hand on the girl's knee but said nothing. Several moments passed.

"After," she continued, "the People were no longer in the Shining Mountains. Long lines of the People struggled westward, leaving our Shining Mountains far behind, most of them forever."

I could see that it was difficult for her, but she went on, as though speaking the words aloud would cleanse her memory of the images.

"I saw the People, after many had sickened and died on the long march, in a sandy, blistered land. There they lived in square lodges made of the flesh of trees. Never moving high into the mountain home in summer. Many more died. Those who were left did not hunt or gather food, but cut our Mother Earth with great knives, trying to make the food grow where it would not.

"The great trees were gone. The Shining Mountains were far to the east. The blue sky was clouded with dust and a strange smoke." She broke off again. I thought she would cry.

"And what did you see then, my daughter?" the old woman asked. Her voice was soft and filled with compassion.

"I saw strange things. Large boxes along straight, wide paths that led nowhere. Box after box, more than could be counted. Men and women lived in them." She looked down into the water at her wavy reflection. "Men and women with skin like mine."

After what seemed like a long time she spoke again.

"Grandmother, I know that I am not born of the People." She fidgeted with the fringe at her sleeve.

"Come. Let us sit nearer to the pool," said Leaves Always Green. They scooted to the edge and dangled their feet in the soothing water. "Daughter, Spirit, you know that I am a Dreamer." The girl nodded.

Spirit! My friend's name is Spirit, I thought. And that's also the word that seems to make the being appear in the Lodge pool.

"Many winters ago, even many winters before you came to us, I dreamed the Great He-She Spirit would send us a new dreamer, one not of the People, who would come to us on a night of great fear. The dreamer's name would be Spirit, in honor of the Great Spirit, who is in us all." The old woman moved her feet slowly in the water. "You have heard the story by our campfires of how the stars fell from the sky twelve winters ago."

"I have heard it many times, Grandmother. Tell me now again."

"It was a night like no other ever known or spoken of by the People. It was near the time of the coming of the winter snows, and we were preparing to leave for our winter camp. We were awakened by howls of alarm from the camp dogs. When we emerged from our lodges we saw the sky was filled with stars streaming down to where the sky meets the earth, as the rain runs down the sides of our lodges in a great storm.

"I was frightened, as were all who lived that night. But I was drawn out of the camp, to this place, by the sound of a child's cries. I heard them first here." She touched herself lightly over her heart. "Later, here." She pointed to her ear. "When I was yet far from this pool I was signalled by a Guide. When I came nearer I saw you, on that ledge of stone." She pointed across the water to the very rock where I had found the little weeping girl.

"I remembered my dream and I knew that the stars were falling to bring you to us, and I was no longer afraid. My dream had said that Spirit would dream with us for a time, then go as she came. I gave you to my daughter, Swift Deer, who was without child. You are of my family."

Spirit said, "My mother has told me that when I was taken into my family my father killed a deer and gave the meat and hide to you. He wanted me to be like you, a Medicine Woman. But I am not, Grandmother. I am not a dreamer, not a good dreamer like you," she protested. "My dreams do not guide. They are of ending, of death. They are of sadness."

And so are mine, I thought.

"You are not a Medicine Woman," Leaves Always Green agreed. "But you are a dreamer. And you must know this thing: All dreams are good. All dreams are guides to those who will listen." She turned Spirit's face toward hers with a thin, weathered hand. "Your dreams are not of ending and death," she said firmly. "They are of change, my child. Do not be sad. Your dreams are of life."

Leaves Always Green hugged Spirit for a long time, holding her with surprising strength. I longed for the old woman's embrace.

Then Leaves Always Green said, "We are here on this earth for a time, receiving what we need from the He-She Spirit. The air, the sunlight, the water, the animals, and the green, growing creatures. Until we are ready to go on. So we will thank the Great Spirit now, by dancing and playing in this holy, healing water."

The old woman took Spirit's hand and pulled her into the warm pool. Soon they were laughing and splashing each other like carefree children. I, too, felt light and happy. I plunged into the water with them.

Spirit reached out to me. I took her hand and found myself suddenly alone, looking across the Lodge's concrete pool at the large boxes that people like me call home.

12

A battered sign dangled from the rusting wire-mesh fence. "MacGregor" announced the faded lettering. Somebody had added the words "Old Lady" with a spray can.

Beyond the fence, and the scraggly-grassed yard which it enclosed, hulked the forbidding house, besieged by vines and gargantuan shrubs which seemed intent on devouring it. Two stately spruce trees protected the porch steps and most of the house from street view. Tentacles of shadow snaked out from these and from the gothic towers which guarded either flank of the spooky old place, inching toward my island of safety in the September sun.

Only an idiot would go in there, a voice inside me said as I recalled the tales I'd heard. But there was no turning back now. Reminding myself of the importance of my mission, I lifted the gate latch and slipped inside the yard.

I willed my legs down the ragged walkway, its huge flagstones tipped erratically by ancient roots. All that talk was just plain silly, kid stuff, I lectured myself as I reached the front entry. I opened the screen door just a crack. Kid stuff or not, my hand trembled as I lifted the tarnished brass knocker on the main door and let it fall.

The sound was puny, not in keeping with my expectation of a haunted house.

Even a witch isn't going to hear that, I thought. I knocked again, harder this time, and waited.

This morning I'd been on my way to the library, hopeful of digging up some information about Colorow and the battle over the hot springs. Who was his band going after? Had they won, as Leaves Always Green foretold? What else happened to Spirit, Colorow, and Leaves Always Green? As I walked, I read a new letter from Jay. That's when Genny caught up with me.

"Hey, what are you reading?" she yelled from a block away, sprinting toward me. A moment later she was panting at my side. "Is it from Jay?"

"Don't be so inhibited, Genny. Say what's on your mind," I said, pulling the two pages out of reach of her grasping hands.

"It is! I was right," she crowed.

"Yes, it is, and it happens to be addressed to Lisa Carey."

"What's it say?" she pleaded, her eyes large and round.

"It says, 'Don't read any of this to Geneva Smith,'" I ad-libbed, but Genny looked so hurt that I quickly admitted I was teasing.

"Really, though, what's it say?" she urged again.

"Well," I started hesitantly, "it's different from the other one."

"Is he coming back? Does he say he loves you?"

108

"Genny!" I said, stomping my foot in irritation. "Would you just let me tell you?"

"Okay," she said brightly.

"He says that school is still fun. He especially likes Anthropology. But things don't seem right with his uncle. He's got a good job, but he drinks all the time and doesn't seem happy."

"Jay?"

"Not Jay. His uncle."

I'd been paraphrasing. Jay's own words were more stark. The situation sounded grim and, although Jay didn't mention it, uncannily like the story of his great-uncle that Jay had told me when we were hiking.

"He says it's uncomfortable living there. He's got some kind of work-study position with the university, and he might look for another place to stay if he can afford it."

"Or come back here," Genny suggested.

Hope surged in me for a moment, but then I came back to earth. "He said school is fun, remember? He'll stay," I told her.

"Maybe. Maybe not."

I didn't answer. Just stashed the letter in my pocket as we rounded the corner and faced the old library. "Oooh, Genny," I whispered darkly, holding her back a little with an extended arm, "don't get too close. You might catch something. Like a love of reading," I said with mock fright.

"Ha, ha, ha."

Inside she followed me to the Colorado Shelf but, before long, drifted to the window. I found a promising title and browsed at a nearby table.

"Genny, listen to this," I said, joining her at her lookout post. "'The Ute Indians have lived in Colorado longer than any other people. They lived in the mountains and occupied much of the plains, too.'"

"Who?" Genny asked.

"The Utes, Genny. The Indians who lived around here before white settlers moved in."

"Oh," she said with just a hint of polite enthusiasm.

"'*But*,'" I paused dramatically, sounding for all the world like a history teacher trying to spark the interest of her class, "'in 1598 the Spanish invaded Ute lands. And then, in 1821, Mexico claimed Ute territory as their own. Even so, the Utes and Mexicans lived peaceably until the United States took control of Colorado in 1848.' That was after the Mexican-American War — you know, the Alamo and all that," I said.

Genny nodded.

"'After gold was discovered near Denver in 1859 great hordes of settlers swept through Ute territory. Prospectors and miners began trespassing on Ute lands. Even after the Treaty of 1868, wherein the United States government promised to the Utes the western one-third of Colorado Territory and no encroachment by whites, the miners wouldn't stay away. The federal government couldn't — or wouldn't — stop them, and in 1873 the Utes were forced to give up more of their treaty land.'"

Genny marked the place on the page with her finger when I stopped for breath, and I was startled to hear her raspy whisper continue where I left off.

"'Utes watched as mining towns sprang up in the mountains,'" she read. "'Not long after Colorado became a state in 1876 cries of *UTES MUST GO!* headlined newspapers in Denver.'"

Genny's eyes widened. "Are they kidding?" she snapped. "The Utes were here first but were thrown off their own land? Where were they supposed to go?" she snorted.

"I don't know, Genny," I said, skimming further on for the answer. In a moment I had it. "Listen to this. It says that in 1879 an Indian agent, Nathan Meeker, and his —"

"There's a town called Meeker," Genny said. "A mountain, too, I think. Keep going."

"— Nathan Meeker and his men were killed by Utes because they were trying to make them live like whites on a reservation somewhere northwest of here. 'Cavalry troops coming to Meeker's aid were attacked and defeated by Chief Colorow'" — my heart skipped a beat — "'then in his sixties, using the same strategy he had used to rout the Arapaho in earlier intertribal battles over the hot springs.'"

There it was, in black and white. Colorow. *Chief* Colorow. And Leaves Always Green was right. He had won his battle for the hot springs. But he was much older in 1879 than the horseman I had seen, the man Spirit married. I read on.

"'In 1880 the Utes were forced onto a desert reservation in Utah. Many died of starvation and disease there, as had many earlier died of grief and privation on the long, forced march westward out of the mountains.'"

I remembered Spirit's dream of the great storm that swept everything before it to the west. Had I read this book first I would swear that I had woven it into some dream of Spirit and Colorow and Leaves Always Green. But I hadn't. My information had come from Spirit first. It still didn't make logical sense, but I was more sure than ever that my visits with Spirit, somehow, were real.

Turning quickly to the index I thumbed through it, and those of some other books as well. There was no other mention of Colorow. And no mention at all of Spirit or Leaves Always Green. I had to know more.

The reference librarian told me the best person to talk to about local history was Lydia MacGregor, a child of one of the first white settler families in the region. And he insisted on writing out meticulously detailed directions to her house, even though I assured him I knew where it was.

I knocked a third time. Still no answer. I felt a curious mixture of relief and disappointment. My retreat had taken me to the porch steps when I heard the sound of a bolt being slid. Then grunting and tugging from the other side of the door. The knob rattled, but the heavy wood door remained fast.

"Hello?" I called meekly into the silence that followed.

There was a moment more of quiet, ruptured suddenly by a sharp, gleeful curse, and the metallic snap of what I took to be another latch device. Before I could prepare myself the door jerked open, as though blasted inward by some unseen force.

A tall, slightly stoop-shouldered woman with blazing white hair stood in the doorway, panting. Muttering something which I could not discern, she slapped lightly at the troublesome latch with a hand covered in splotchy skin three sizes too large.

"Mrs. MacGregor?" I squeaked as she turned a wild-eyed gaze on me. "I'm from . . . My name is Lisa," I started again.

"I can only give a little," she protested as she fumbled through a brocaded coin purse which appeared in her hand from nowhere. "I'm no longer employed, you know," she added.

I was confused. "I'm Lisa Carey, from —" I noticed Mrs. MacGregor was smiling now, a quarter clamped between her thumb and forefinger. I refused the coin with a stop-sign hand. "I'm not collecting money or anything," I said.

"You're not?"

"I'm from up the street," I said, as though that explained my presence on this ancient woman's doorstep.

"Oh," she laughed, carefree as a child. "I wonder why you're here, then?" she asked, snapping the purse shut on the redeposited coin. Before I could answer, she said, "I thought you were some kind of collection person. Except for my young man, they're the only ones who come anymore." She hunched forward a little. "Mostly old ladies," she whispered conspiratorially as she reached to scratch her enormous old-lady ear. "Nothing better to do, I guess," she concluded, dismissing them with a disdainful wave of her hand. "But you look more interesting." She snatched a hand-carved wooden cane from out of the shadows. "Come in, come in," she invited, stepping aside to let me pass.

"Sure," I said, though I was anything but.

"You needn't be afraid. I'm not such a witch as they say," she announced matter-of-factly, and deftly poked the wooden screen door open with the tip of her gnarled cane.

I grabbed the knob of the door and listened to the song of the uncoiling spring as I opened it wider. "Just for a few minutes," I said, as though the words might protect me from unknown dangers.

"Your name again?" Mrs. MacGregor asked as I stepped into the cavernous hallway.

"Lisa Carey," I repeated.

"Good," she said.

Another poke with her cane, and the door slammed shut behind me.

13

I stood motionless, nearly blind in the dark interior, as the *swish* of Mrs. MacGregor's skirt and the *plunk* of her cane moved confidently past me, then stopped a few feet further on.

"This way," she called like a troop leader on a scout hike. "Follow me."

We traveled down a dark corridor and turned through the second door on the left. I worked to memorize the route in case I needed to make a quick escape.

"This is the sitting room," Mrs. MacGregor said.

The sitting room was high-ceilinged and the walls were mostly covered with old-fashioned, flowered wallpaper. Heavy draperies came almost to the floor along one wall. A slit of light at the middle showed the windows to be nearly as tall, with low sills barely a foot off the floor. I felt like I was the only taker on a tour of haunted houses.

"Kind of dark in here, don't you think?" Mrs. MacGregor asked.

"A little," I answered. Oppressive would have been a better word.

She went over to the window nearest her and tugged on a cord. Slowly, the coils of heavy cloth moved aside. It hardly made a difference. The roof and a large spruce blocked most of the weak afternoon light that remained on this side of the house.

"Well, set yourself down." Mrs. MacGregor directed me to a worn, overstuffed chair near the uncovered window. The cushion was surprisingly comfortable, but I felt swallowed up by the high back and the big arm rests. They were frayed. I pulled nervously at the threads.

"It's old," Mrs. MacGregor said.

I put my hands in my lap, embarrassed. "What is?" I asked

"The chair. The house. Me. We're all old. The house and I were born the same year: 1907. That makes us eighty-eight."

"That is pretty old," I said, trying to be agreeable. Then quickly added, "For a house," I mean.

"You don't think it's pretty old for a person? Feels old sometimes, let me tell you. Give me some credit," she said.

"I just meant —"

"Oh, quit being so polite," she growled. "I'm old, you're young. Nothing to be embarrassed about, either way."

"I'm sorry."

"There you go again," she said. "Land sakes, by the time you're done apologizing I'll be dead." She settled back into her chair again. "Anyway, I don't care much for the decor anymore." She waved her cane accusingly at the room in general. "Dungeon decor, I call it. But, I don't get callers much and I don't have money to fix things up, either. What's an old lady to do?"

116

"I think it looks . . ."

Sirens and lights went off in my brain.

". . . kind of . . ."

I didn't want another balling out.

". . . kind of . . . dingy?"

"Good for you!" she exclaimed. "That came out about as easy as honey from a jar on a winter morning, didn't it?" She laughed, rocking forward and slapping her cane on the rug. "Oh. My." She caught her breath. "Next time it'll be easier."

Old lady or not, witch or not, I could see that Mrs. MacGregor had been a beautiful woman. And still was. Winter sky blue eyes accented her warm, open face. And her soft white hair, billowing high over her forehead and swept back into a grandmotherly bun, inspired anything but terror.

"So, Lisa Carey, what brings you here today?"

I started to explain about the research I was doing and how the reference librarian had directed me to her as the definitive source of information about local history. But before I got very far Mrs. MacGregor suddenly snapped her fingers.

"Tea and cake," she fairly shouted.

"Pardon?"

"We must have tea and cake."

She ushered me back through the house into a large, bright, old-fashioned kitchen. The last rays of sun streamed in through a wall of windows, filling the room with light. Potted plants hung from the ceiling and crammed every inch of window sill. A porcelain sink hung heavy on one wall and white wooden cabinets lined the space on either side. The refrigerator had an electrical cord extending from behind, but judging from the appliance's squat shape and scratched enamel finish it must have been the first model out after iceboxes. A sturdy wooden table with carved legs and two extender leaves stood in the middle of the floor. A large poster of Albert Einstein was taped to one wall and his gleeful Santa Claus eyes watched over the room.

"*This* is where I *live*," Mrs. MacGregor announced with pride.

She quickly placed flour, milk, eggs, honey, and spices on the table. It seemed to me that Mrs. MacGregor had dropped about thirty years since entering the room.

"Tom made this table. He was my husband," she grunted as she measured flour into a mixing bowl.

"I could help," I offered.

"Good," she said, handing the bowl to me. She pointed to the spices with one hand. "Quarter teaspoon each," she said, reaching for the egg carton with the other. "He died young. In a road accident. Made these chairs, too."

"I'm sorry," I said.

"Why? They're perfectly good. Lasted fifty years and still going strong. Better than that junk you see in the stores today, I'll tell you." She broke two eggs into another bowl.

"No, the chairs and table are beautiful. I mean I'm sorry about . . . about your husband dying." I thought about my father. How I hated for anyone to bring it up.

"Oh. Well," she said, resting her hands on the table for an instant. "I'm sorry, too."

"I didn't mean to —"

"Ah-ah!" she ordered, holding up a finger that stopped me in mid-sentence. "Don't spoil a perfectly good conversation. Besides which, I don't get much opportunity to brag on Tom. Better add a pinch of salt there." She picked a long wooden spoon from a pottery jar next to the stove, and beat the eggs while she talked.

"He was a good man. And he led as good a life as he knew how in the time he had. It was a long time ago." She added the milk and honey and mixed the wet ingredients with a vengeance. "Tom was a talented craftsman," she said, "already well established when we married. I was a twenty-eight year old school teacher. 'Old maid' they called it back then.

"Do you have any children?" I asked.

"Catherine was our only child." She rested the spoon in the bowl and pointed a bony finger toward a small, bleached-out photo I hadn't noticed before on the wall, just below the Einstein poster. A young, dark-haired woman with a full face and a smile tugging at the corners of her thin lips. She reminded me of the Mona Lisa.

"Does she live here in Indian Springs?"

"She died when she was thirty. Cancer. She was a teacher, too. Lived here with me until she died." She stopped mixing. "Strange, a child dying before her mother."

Mrs. MacGregor passed her bowl to me. While I mixed the wet and dry ingredients together and put them in a pan

119

she provided, she worked at lighting an ancient gas oven with the longest wooden match I had ever seen. I hoped the stove wouldn't blow up.

Waiting for the oven to come to temperature, Mrs. MacGregor studied my face as if she were devouring everything inside my head. It didn't feel intrusive, though. I kind of liked it, even.

"Tell me about yourself, Lisa."

In a flood of words I told her about our move to Indian Springs, the ongoing battles with my mother, my father's death and how I missed him.

"I missed Catherine and Tom terribly," she said. "They died within two years of each other. At first I wouldn't believe they were gone. I absolutely refused. Then, I dreamed about them a lot."

"Me, too," I interrupted. "Nightmares." She nodded.

"I felt angry, too," she said. "Angry that they left me."

"What did you do?" I asked, hoping that she might have some magic answer for me.

"Well, what could I do? What can any of us do? For a while I was pretty mixed up — begging God to bring them back one day, blaming Him, and them, and everybody else the next. That's no good," she said. "Makes you old and bitter. Besides, what's the use? I couldn't hold on forever. I couldn't grieve forever. And I knew that neither of them would have wanted me to.

"And then, of course, Mr. Einstein helped." She pointed to the poster. "Do you know what he said when a friend of his died? He said that death signifies nothing. That the distinction between past, present, and future is just a stubborn illusion." She put the pan in the oven and closed the oven door gently as she turned to look at me. "So, I put all those things together, and I let go."

"But don't you still miss them?" I asked.

"I do," she said. "Not in the same way as at first. Not most of the time. Not even very often. But in certain moments." She walked slowly back to her chair and sat down. "If I had my 'druthers, Lisa, I'd have Tom and Catherine here to share tea and cake with us today." She tapped the table top with the point of her forefinger, as though she were calling them this instant. "But we don't always get to have our 'druthers. And hanging on wouldn't mean I loved them any more. Just like letting go didn't mean I loved them any less." She placed her hands quietly in her lap. "My mother used to say, 'Things always work out for the best. Everything is a blessing.'"

"Do you think that's true?" I asked. "That everything is a blessing?"

She looked at me with those steady blue eyes. "Yes," she said. "I do."

A moment later Mrs. MacGregor leaped from her chair as though it had been electrified, grabbed her cane, and — carrying the stick as though her purpose were to deliver it to someone else, someone who needed it — fairly ran through an arched doorway made narrow by two lumpy burlap sacks. I heard the rattle of loose glass panes as the rear door banged open, and the creak of another screen door spring.

"Come and see my little garden, Lisa," she called.

Little garden? The whole backyard was a jungle of plants of every size and shape and flowers of every color. I caught up to her as she was calling the roll.

"Kale, collards, beets, carrots, beans, pumpkin, tomatoes, corn," she announced, counting off each with the tip of her pointer cane. "I grow most of the vegetables and herbs I use. My young man helps, of course. Couldn't do without him."

She stopped at a thick stand of knee-high plants, slowly lowered herself to one knee with the help of her cane, and began yanking the sprigs out and tossing them into the lap of her cotton dress, which draped the ground in front of her. "We'll take some of this peppermint for our tea. You get some, too."

I had never picked my own tea before. It was fun. Soon my hands and all the air around us were drenched with the sharp fragrance of mint.

"That's enough. More than enough," Mrs. MacGregor said. "I'll get the rest later on and dry them. It won't be long until the frost and the end of the growing season. Then I'll have a lovely blanket of snow to look at. And a cupboard full of delicious peppermint tea to keep me warm all winter long."

To my surprise, Mrs. MacGregor became an actual old lady as she tried to get up off her knees, and she seemed grateful when I moved close enough for her to grab hold of my arm. "That ground gets a little further down every year," she said.

A few minutes later hot ginger cake and steaming cups of peppermint tea sat on the table. The sweet and spicy flavors blended deliciously and I told her so. She said her young man loves ginger cake.

"I'll bet he does," I said. I was beginning to wonder about Mrs. MacGregor and her young man.

"And the kids, too," she said, refusing to take the bait. "At Halloween I bake spice cookies and meet them at the door dressed as a witch. Don't even need much makeup." Her eyes shone as she described her costume. "Just black face paint on my lips and take out my uppers." She laughed unselfconsciously as she grabbed her front tooth and wiggled half the teeth in the roof of her mouth.

"Kids love to scare themselves," she said." And they love a mystery, too. I provide an opportunity for both. They make up stories about me, that I'm a witch or a ghost, because I'm old and my house is old and I never leave the place. At least not by the front," she whispered. "I spend my time in the garden, and most things I need I have delivered. The only time the kids see me is at Halloween." She sipped her tea noisily. "I don't suppose you're scared of me, though, are you?"

I laughed. "No. Not anymore, anyway. In fact, if you'd let me, I'd like to help with your garden."

"Oh, goodness my!" she exclaimed. "Why that would be wonderful. I do believe we'd get along. And I could certainly use the help."

"What about your young man?" I asked.

"Oh, I don't think he'll be coming for a while." She pushed another piece of cake at me. "Now, do tell me why you're here."

Soon I was deep into it, telling her how interested I was in learning from her about Colorow and the Utes that had camped near the river so many years ago. Anything she could tell.

To my surprise she explained that she was in the process of writing her memoirs for the town Historical Society, that she knew "quite a little bit" about Colorow, and that she would be glad to tell me anything she could. "I'm a little crippled," she said with a nod to the cane hanging by its crook from the table edge, "but there's nothing wrong with my memory. Most days," she laughed, settling back in her chair.

"My parents were among the first white settlers in this valley. They came the year they were married, 1885. By that time Chief Colorow was very old, but he still returned here every summer to hunt. His life wasn't easy. By then his people lived like prisoners on the reservation the government stuck them on in Utah. Most of his friends had either starved, been killed, or committed suicide. He was gentle and good-hearted by nature, but he couldn't abide the whites settling in on land promised forever to the Utes.

"My mother, who knew him because he came to her house to eat *her* spice cake every summer, said he was a large man. He was born Comanche, you know, but was adopted by the Utes after being captured as a baby in one of the intertribal raids. Because of his Comanche heritage he was taller and redder than the Utes. His Indian name was Too-p'-weets. Colorow was the name that the white men knew him by. It's a contraction of 'Colorado,' which means 'the red.' He was made a chief after winning an important battle against the Arapaho over the hot springs located right here in town. Doesn't that speak well of the Ute people, and of Colorow, too, making him a chief and him not even born a Ute?" she exclaimed. "I should say so," she answered. "Much later, in about '78 or '79, he defeated a cavalry force at Milk Creek. Up by Meeker." She pointed over her shoulder as though it were across the street. "But fate was against him. He and his people couldn't keep the settlers out of these lands forever." She licked her finger and dabbed crumbs up from her plate.

"I always thought it very sad," she said. "He wasn't just some name in a book. He was a real, living human being. He loved his life and his people just as you and I love ours. He loved this spot in particular and came back here every summer on horseback with his friends. They set up their teepees. Beautiful things, my mother said, made of red elk skins.

"The last time he came, my mother said, was the year the swimming pool was built. That would be in '88. He died in December of that year. I've often wondered," she said, "how he felt about them taking his healing water and turning it into a swimming pool."

"How old was he when he died?" I gathered up the cups and saucers and carried them over to the sink.

"Oh, I think he must have been about seventy-five when he died," Mrs. MacGregor said. "Why?"

"I've been reading. I'm just trying to put together all the pieces."

"Have you heard about the legend?"

"What legend?" I said.

"There's an old legend about Colorow. Maybe true, maybe not. It says that when Colorow was a young man he married a white girl who had been raised by his tribe after she was found wandering on a mountain trail alone."

"The night of the falling stars," I murmured involuntarily.

"What's that?"

I shook my head. "Nothing," I said. "Go on."

Mrs. MacGregor's sharp eyes narrowed, but she continued with her story. "They loved to travel together, Colorow and his bride. But she died young, barely more than a child. Right near here. She was riding away from the hot springs and fell from a spooked horse. Many years later, when Colorow came that last summer, the legend says, he stood by the newly built pool early of an evening. 'Spirit!' he called. That was his lady's name. And her form rose before him like the mists from the water."

I could hardly believe my ears.

"Once when I was young, about your age I'd say, I sat by the pool myself one evening. I spoke her name, too, just the way the legend said. I wanted to see what would happen."

"What did happen?" I asked.

"I thought I saw a girl in the water. She had long blond hair that floated all around her. It nearly took my breath away. But, as suddenly as I saw her, she was gone. It must have been my imagination, don't you think?"

"I don't know," I told her honestly.

The first frost came that very night. I wondered if Mrs. MacGregor's garden survived.

14

The girl on the ledge, Leave Always Green's granddaughter, Colorow's wife, the being in the pool. Were they all one and the same? And did they really exist? I reviewed the evidence from the beginning, laying it out like pieces in a puzzle.

First, my own repeated encounters with a being in the pool, encounters which transported me to a time and place and people in the past that I experienced as utterly real. Second, the physical evidence: my sore shin, the broken railing, the reports of someone jumping into the pool. Third, and most important, the things that I "knew" before I otherwise could have: Colorow, seen and heard with my own eyes and ears, described and named in a book I only read later on, and then again in Mrs. MacGregor's story; Spirit's "storm" dream, known to me before I read at the library about the forced march to Utah and the reservation; and finally, Spirit's name, and her connection with a man called Colorow.

And now, the legend of Spirit inhabiting the pool at the Lodge.

I had wondered once before if there was a connection between Spirit and the girl in the water, when I first heard Leaves Always Green speak Spirit's name. But the girl in the pool was always hazy, ghost-like. A girl, I was sure, but not one I could draw a picture of. I could not even have said whether she was five or fifteen or twenty-five. Still, she did have the same blond hair as Spirit. And each time the water spirit disappeared, I found myself in the past, with Spirit near at hand. And Spirit was the one, the only one perhaps, who could see and hear me. Also, touching hands with the water-being seemed to be the mechanism which actually propelled me into the past. And touching the hand of Spirit in the past, I suddenly realized, always brought me back to the present. And, of course, Mrs. MacGregor's experiment at the pool, and my own experience as well, involved calling the name "Spirit." Which is exactly what Colorow did, and he was obviously calling Spirit herself.

The girl in the water. Spirit. One and the same.

Somehow I have traveled through time and met people from the past. People who really lived. And died.

My thoughts raced furiously, examining pieces of the puzzle that didn't yet seem to fit, searching for others still missing. Like the meteors, the bear, the spooked horse. And Spirit. If it is her in the pool, why is she there? And why does she always disappear just when I get close?

Spirit died near the hot springs. A spooked horse, Mrs. MacGregor said. But my nightmare connected Spirit's death with the Bear Dance. Of course, I've already learned that Spirit *didn't* die at the Bear Dance. And now her spirit or body or *some*thing inhabits the hot springs, and has for more than a hundred years. And calls me, leads me, into the past.

But why? To save her life, as I thought earlier? If so, obviously not by warning her about a nightmare. For a reason, surely, but a sadness deep inside told me it was not to save her life. Why then? And, for that matter, why me?

Clang!

I clutched my aching head and knew that the sound was not inside, but in my ears. I looked around: commotion. Kids leaving the room. I was in History class. Or had been. Forty-five minutes had gone by and I couldn't have told you one thing that was said. The last few bodies scuttled out the door.

Almost immediately the flow reversed itself. Color and sound and movement filled the room. I stayed in my seat, too light-headed to get up. Someone came down the aisle from the back. He turned, looked down at me, waiting. Probably his regular seat.

"Joining our class today, Miss . . . uh . . ." He snapped his thumb across his middle finger, trying to spark the memory of my name.

"Carey," I answered automatically, still disoriented. The finger popping stopped.

"Yes. Lisa Carey, if I remember correctly." It was Mr. Burrows. "Well, I hate to be the one to break the news, but this is not Biology, Lisa."

"I already had Biology today, huh?" I said, not quite sure whether I was making a statement or asking a question.

"Yes. Very good of you to remember. However, this is Earth Sciences and the bell is about to ring. Don't you have some place to be?" he asked.

"Uh, yes, sir," I said. "But it's just study hall. Could I sit in today?"

"Sit in?" he echoed, as though it were a hard question. "I don't know. You'd need a pass."

"I'm sure I could get one. Ms. Butler wouldn't care."

"I'm showing a filmstrip on meteors. Are you a special fan of meteors?" he asked, a touch of sarcasm in his voice.

"Yes," I answered. I was. I certainly was. "Really," I insisted. "I like them a lot. I can stay, can't I?" I sounded like an orphan out of some Dickens novel.

"I can hardly refuse such an eager student. I hope your enthusiasm is catching." He nodded toward the door. "Better hurry and get that pass," he said.

When I returned, Mr. Burrows was pulling a screen down from its nest in the ceiling. I found a new seat towards the back.

"Who has seen a shooting star?" Mr. Burrows asked. Most of the students raised their hands. "That was a trick question, actually. Anybody know why it was a trick question?" All of the hands dropped but one. "Miss Bronowski?"

"No one could have seen a shooting star, because there is no such thing."

"That's right, Melinda. Thank you. What we commonly call shooting stars are, actually, meteors. Perhaps some of you knew that." He paused, but if

131

anyone knew, they weren't letting on. "We call them shooting stars, even today, most of us, because that's what they look like, stars shooting across the heavens. And, because until relatively recently, no one knew anything about what they really are, the phenomenon we now refer to as meteors." A hand shot up to my left. "Yes. Mr. Richardson?"

"What is a meteor? Actually." Mr. Burrows either didn't notice his mimicry or didn't care. "Is it like what made that big hole in the ground in Arizona?"

"Have you been to Barringer Crater, Tim?"

"What's that?" Tim asked.

"It's that big hole in the ground," Mr. Burrows said dryly. "In Arizona."

"Oh. No, but I saw that old movie, *Star Man*." A few nods of recognition from the class caused Tim to undergo a strange transformation. "I must go . . . to . . . where was it? . . . to . . . uh . . . that big hole . . . in Arizona," he said, talking stiffly and tilting his head like a mechanical dog. Apparently he had become Star Man. The class enjoyed it and a few tried to egg him on, but Mr. Burrows pulled us all back to earth.

"To answer your question, Tim," he said, addressing the strange visitor from another planet as though he were just another student in the class, "the word 'meteor' comes from the Greek *meteoron* and later the Latin *meteorum* meaning 'thing in the air.'" He quickly scrawled the words on the board. "Meteors are solid bits of matter of relatively small size, actually. Most are no larger than grains of sand or small pebbles. When these enter the earth's atmosphere they heat up from the friction, so hot that they actually burn up in the process. Some larger ones don't burn up completely and they strike the planet's surface. When a meteor makes it to the ground it's called a meteorite. The crater you refer to in Arizona was formed about 25,000 years ago by a rather large meteorite.

"Any other . . . questions . . . Tim?" Mr. Burrows did a very good imitation of Tim doing Star Man and, judging by the clapping and whistles which followed, won over most of Tim's fans.

"Now, anyone who has spent much time out of doors at night knows that shooting stars, so-called, are not such a rare sight. On a clear night in a dark area you might see five to ten per hour. But, on fairly frequent occasions, actually, they are more numerous. Such an event is called a meteor *shower*. Has anyone here seen a meteor shower?" A few hands went up. "How about the shower this past August eleventh and twelfth?" Some of the hands dropped, leaving just mine and two others.

"That one is known as the Perseid Shower because the meteors appear to be coming from the constellation Perseus. As I said earlier, they are just small bits of dust — from a comet, actually — burning up in earth's atmosphere.

"Many meteor displays, the Perseids included, are quite predictable, returning at the same time every year. This is an illusion of sorts, insofar as it is not the meteors' return, actually, but the earth's return through the comet's debris-filled orbit at the same time each year which causes them to appear. Now. Who can tell me what a meteor *storm* is?"

I raised my hand.

"Miss Carey?" Half the class turned at the sound of my name. An intruder, discovered. "Quiet, please," Mr. Burrows said, and the buzz settled down. "Lisa?"

"Well, I would say a meteor storm would be like a tremendously intense shower. You know, the sky just filled with stars falling everywhere at once. Like a fireworks display, only no sound."

"That's very good, Lisa. Very good." He tossed a piece of chalk in the air and caught it several times as he walked across the front of the room. "And who has seen such a storm?"

. . . The night sky is on fire. The whole sky is alive with bright flashes of light . . . Stars fall like snow in a blizzard. Hundreds and hundreds at once . . .

"Lisa?" Mr. Burrow's voice startled me. Hadn't I just finished answering? I looked around the room. No hand was raised but mine.

"What was the question?" I wasn't exactly stalling. I wasn't sure if I had blanked out again or something.

"I asked if anyone's seen a meteor storm," he said.

I was in a jam. I couldn't explain the one I'd seen. He'd want to know when and where.

I imagined myself up in front of the class, telling everyone, Sure, I saw a meteor storm. Just a few weeks ago, in fact. Right here in Indian Springs. They would be amazed. Especially Mr. Burrows, who would point out that there wasn't any meteor storm a few weeks ago. This didn't seem to be the time or place to get into a show-and-tell on time travel.

"I'm sorry," I said quietly. "I made a mistake." My reply faded out as the laughter began. I sank into my seat, feeling the blood rush to my face. Mr. Burrows did his best to rescue me.

"No shame in that," he said. "But let me just say that if you had, you would be the envy of us all. The envy, I might say, of a large portion of the professional astronomy community. Such storms occur only a few times each century and are to a large degree unpredictable, unfortunately. But this filmstrip will give us an idea of what it would be like." He fiddled with some levers on the projector and, by turning off the lights and closing the blinds, switched the room into inky blackness. "Now, on with the show."

Light danced onto the white screen. Drawings of shooting stars and pictures of comets appeared, a disembodied voice talking all the while about the gas and dust nature of comets, and their orbits around the sun that bring us the meteor displays. A lot of it was a rehash, with illustrations, of what Mr. Burrows had already said.

"Although meteors have been noted since the beginning of recorded history," the narrator continued, "the science of meteors did not really begin until 1833, after what was perhaps the most incredible meteor storm known to man. In November of that year hundreds of thousands of meteor tracks were observed by individuals through much of the United States." A crude drawing of what looked like a fireworks burst filled the screen. The image startled me. "One observer estimated that tens of thousands flashed across the sky in an hour's time. This was an occurrence of the annual Leonid meteor shower, now thought to have a periodic return of intense displays on an approximate thirty-three year cycle."

Another artist's representation came onto the screen. Again it was shockingly familiar.

"Many people were frightened. They didn't know they were seeing only particles of dust. They thought that the very stars were falling and would hit them. Many thought they were witnessing the end of the world."

I was no longer watching the screen up front, but had tuned instead to the one inside my head. I saw again the countless streams of light racing across the night sky, felt the paralysis of breath, the tingles of fear on my scalp and spine. I thought of little Spirit, alone in the mountains, the sky falling all around her. Her small face, twisted and shiny from crying. Her dress torn and dirty from her fall down the hillside. I could understand her terror and well believe the people of the time would be disoriented, bewildered, and just plain scared. For I, a supposedly educated, sophisticated person of the twentieth century had been frightened out of my wits.

The tiny bell on the sound track sounded. The screen and the narrator moved on to other meteor facts.

Was this the meteor storm I had witnessed? I quickly put together a chronology of events. Colorow came to the hot springs in 1888 Mrs. MacGregor had said, when he was about seventy-five years old. Also, he fought the soldiers at Milk Creek in 1879, when he was thought to be about sixty-five. By both accounts he would have been born in about 1813. I found Spirit when she was maybe four years old. If that was, in fact, during the storm of 1833, then twelve years later when I saw her at the Bear Dance she would have been sixteen and Colorow thirty-two. It all seemed about right.

"Don't miss our next chance to view the Leonid shower," Mr. Burrows said as the lights fluttered back to life. "That's the same one that produced the storm described in 1833." There was a sudden buzz of excitement. "No, no," he said. "This one will only be a light shower. Probably about twenty meteors per hour."

The bell rang. "So bundle up," he said as students trampled each other to the door, "and go out in the early morning hours of November 17 if you want a first-hand experience." I don't think too many people heard him. But I did. And something about it bothered me. Scared me, even.

"How'd you like the class, Lisa?" Mr. Burrows said. I tried to shake my fear off.

"Very exciting. Thanks for letting me sit in."

"Any time. You were really into it. That makes teaching more fun." I nodded, and began collecting my things. "In fact," he continued, "I couldn't help noticing your rapt expression during the filmstrip. I almost began to wonder if maybe you *had* seen a meteor storm, or something like it." His cool gaze skittered across my face.

I wanted to tell him about it. I wanted to tell *someone* and he was an expert, and a person who was intensely interested, too. But I couldn't. He wouldn't understand that I'd seen the one in 1833. He'd think I was nuts.

"Just wishful thinking," I said.

"I can understand that. I'd give almost anything to see something like the 1833 storm."

"Me, too."

I headed toward the door. Genny's face was framed by the little window. She ducked back out of sight as I came near. I knew she'd been trying to listen to our conversation, but I doubted she could have heard anything much through the heavy steel door.

"Hey, don't miss that Leonid shower," Mr. Burrows said as I reached for the door handle. "The next storm isn't expected until around 1998 or 1999, but you never can be sure when you'll see something really spectacular."

"Thanks again. The film was great."

As soon as I stepped out the door, Genny pounced. "Why weren't you in study hall? Were you having a tryst with Mr. Tall, Dark, and Handsome?"

She was biting dreamily into an apple a second after she asked the question and it just didn't seem to call for an entirely serious reply. So I smiled and raised my eyebrows as if to say, You could be onto something. Something big.

"Listen, I saw the two of you in there," she said in a more conspiratorial voice. "What's going on?" I was feeling alive and happy and a bit like catching Genny's nose poked where it didn't belong.

"Why, whatever do you mean, Geneva?"

She pulled at her hair. "Come *on*, Lisa," she demanded in her most forlorn tone. But I was enjoying myself too much to stop.

"Do get hold of yourself, dear. What you witnessed was only, oh how shall I say it, *une petite tête-à-tête*," I said, doing my best to flutter my eyelids.

"Just a little chat? An intimate little chat?"

"*Oui*. A little chat." I smiled. Deliciously.

She laughed. "You're just teasing me, aren't you?" I didn't say a word. Just kept staring her right in those big tawny eyes. "Aren't you?" she repeated, but by that time I was five steps down the hall.

"I really feel it's something private," I said as she zoomed to catch up. "You know, just between me and Mister . . . that is . . . Robert." It was fun watching her squirm for a moment, but I knew she was distraught when she threw the apple she'd taken only that single bite out of into the waste can.

"Lisa Carey, you'd better tell me what's going on, sister."

"Nothing's going on," I finally told her honestly. She wasn't convinced. "Okay, okay," I said. "But I warn you, you don't want to hear this." I knew what she *wanted* to hear.

"Try me."

"I stayed to see a filmstrip." Her face was a study in blankness. "About meteors. He showed it in Earth Sciences." Not a flicker of response. She was obviously waiting for the whole truth and nothing but.

"What about *after* class?" she said, cocking her head to one side.

"We talked about meteors some more. He's really interested in them, I guess." I was beginning to worry she'd get a crick in her neck. "That's it," I shrugged.

"Oh." Her face dropped like someone who's just heard she almost won the lottery. "That's it?" she asked. I nodded, amazed at how guilty I could feel for not living up to my friend's fantasies. "Oh," she repeated as bleakly as before.

But when I left her at her door she said, "You know, I'm very interested in meteors myself, actually."

Poor Mr. Burrows.

15

"He doesn't sound so happy in Boulder anymore. Genny thinks maybe he'll come back home soon," I told Mrs. MacGregor later that day.

I had rushed over to her house after school. I found Mrs. MacGregor in the back, pulling dead corn stalks out of the garden. She was huffing and puffing. I was afraid she might hurt herself, and I insisted on pulling the rest. Some of them were plenty tough, and I was puffing myself by the time I had an arm load. During breathers I'd told her about Jay's latest letter.

"He's got to find his own way," she said. "And he will, if I know Jay Redpath at all."

"You *know* him?"

"Yes, ma'am, I certainly do. He's my young man I believe I've mentioned to you." My face turned hot. "Don't worry, Lisa. I wouldn't pass along anything you say to me. What's said here, stays here." She piled the flimsy skeletons of once-lush zucchini plants in a heap.

"How'd you meet?" I asked.

"Oh, goodness!" she exclaimed. "He's been delivering my groceries since he was big enough to carry the bag. And for the last few years he's been helping me with the garden." She leaned on her cane. "I guess I brag on a little about how I grow most all my own food but, truth is, I finally got too old to do it all on my own."

I called a short truce with the corn and studied her sweet, determined face. I hoped with all my heart that I would be as strong of body and of soul as Old Lady MacGregor when I was her age. I promised to help her with the spring planting. It seemed like a first step down that road.

"Good," she said. "That'd be good."

Late that night, tired and muscle-sore but infused with adrenalin, I grabbed a warm jacket and hurried out into the frosty street. I was on my way to visit Spirit. Spirit and Leaves Always Green and Colorow.

And I was thinking about Einstein. I didn't know much about his theory of relativity. In fact, nothing, except that there was such a thing, and that it had something to do with time and space not being what they seemed to be. My father had gotten a book once from the library about parallel universes. Not science fiction, either. I tried to read it. I got far enough to know that it was somebody's theory that there are lots of worlds all around us, which we can't see. It got me to thinking now — maybe Spirit and Leaves Always Green and all the Utes are right here beside me, living their lives at the same time as I am.

It seemed preposterous. But no more preposterous than that I saw a meteor storm that happened in 1833. I didn't understand the how of it. All I knew was that somehow and for some purpose my life was connected with those people's lives. And that I must keep returning to them until I had accomplished whatever it was I was supposed to do.

"Spirit," I called. "Spirit." I looked for the familiar figure under the water. Spirit came to the surface, smiled her peaceful smile, and invited me in as usual. "Spirit? You *are* Spirit, aren't you?" I asked. "The little girl I found over there on the rock ledge?" I pointed beyond the pool fence, past the streetlights and silent buildings to the ledge on the hidden hillside.

But Spirit didn't speak. She didn't nod or show any sign that she had heard or understood. She just waved me to come into the water.

I jumped, ready for anything, I thought.

It was a dark morning, the usual brilliance of the mountain sky shrouded with sagging, slate-grey clouds. Heavy, wet snow blanketed the ground. The only sound I heard was the shrill, staccato bark of a far off coyote.

At the Ute camp everything was in motion. Women were dismantling the teepees and packing gear on sled-like contraptions. The men rounded up the horses and attached the sleds to them with poles and cord.

The Nuu-chi were preparing to move their camp. They were leaving this place, going to a lower, warmer area for the winter. I wondered if I would ever see them again.

Of course you will, I told myself. The Utes have been making this winter trek ever since you found Spirit, and for centuries before that, according to Jay. They'll come back in the spring, when the bears come out of hibernation.

And with the total lack of control I seemed to have over the timing of my visits, that might easily be the next time I showed up here.

I wandered through what was left of camp, looking for Spirit. Everyone was busy. There was no idle conversation. The coyote yipped again, and was answered this time by a chorus of camp dogs. The howls sent prickles up my spine.

A tall, thick-trunked pine, stark and singular beyond the edge of the camp, seemed to beckon to me. Trudging toward it through heavy snow I saw that Spirit stood at its base. Beside her was a small mound of skins or furs. She raised her hand in greeting.

As I drew nearer to my friend and the rugged, red-barked tree, waves of sadness washed over me. Like the cold, the feeling seeped into me with every step, but it was not until I reached her that I saw the frail figure lying beneath a single furred skin. It was Leaves Always Green.

"Please, Grandmother, I will help you to the travois. The horse will pull you and you will come with us." Spirit's face was stained with tears. "You will tell me stories all winter in our warm lodge."

"No, my daughter. I will winter here," Leaves Always Green answered. A gentle smile transfigured her old face.

"But you will die, Grandmother," Spirit said.

"Yes, and so shall we all. The owl called my name. It is a good time. Do not hold me here with your tears, my child."

Leaves Always Green looked at me. I felt invited and I moved closer. She turned her attention back to Spirit. Gently, she lifted Spirit's face so that she could look into her eyes.

"What have you dreamed, Daughter?"

Spirit let out a breath, whether of relief or resignation I could not tell. "I do not understand, Grandmother. I see no future for me. I see Colorow. He is an old man, proud but sad. He stands by a pool of steaming water, and the water is trapped all around with a strange stone. He reaches his arms over the water as far as he can stretch them. 'Spirit,' he calls. His heart cries, Grandmother. That is all. I see no more. Why does he call me by the water that is captured by stone?"

"Your dream is your guide," Leaves Always Green said. "When your cycle is over, do not cling to Mother Earth." Her words came slowly. It was an effort for her to speak. "Your friend who brought you to me long ago is here."

"Yes, Grandmother," Spirit said.

"She will guide you, also." Large snowflakes floated down around us. Leaves Always Green looked up at me again. "Come," she said to me, and indicated with her eyes the place beside Spirit. We knelt there, the two of us, by the old woman's side. Somewhere far off the coyote sang.

"Soon I will join the others who have gone before. We complete our circle and go to the Spirit Light." Her gaze traveled back and forth between my face and Spirit's.

"And this body, which is tired, will soon return to the earth. Our Mother will continue her dance of seasons."

She rested for a few moments. Her breath was shallow. "Do not grieve for me, dear Daughter. Grieve for yourself a little while. And when that time is done, grieve no more. All is as it should be."

She stroked Spirit's chin lightly with a frail hand, then rested her calming gaze on me. "Do not hold others with your grief, or death becomes a horror. The snowflake falls to the ground, melts in its season, and greens the earth. Snowflakes do not fear the spring."

Her face glowed with a light so intense I thought I could only be imagining it. But I think Spirit must have seen it, too, because her face mirrored the joy I felt inside.

"And now, you must go," Leaves Always Green said to me. She took my hand in her own. For a moment I thought I might be in heaven. "Go," she said.

The next thing I knew I was standing on the balcony, looking into the sleepy hot springs pool.

16

"Letters! Mail call!" Sandy waved a pair of envelopes in the air, singing the words as she came in the door.

I sat in the window seat, looking into the heart of town, to where I was pretty sure I'd last seen Spirit and Leaves Always Green. Nearly two weeks had gone by. I hadn't returned to the past, not since Leaves Always Green died. And I hadn't let go. The next morning I'd wandered around the Lodge area and its surroundings, trying to identify landmarks common to the two worlds. I located the very rock ledge on which I first found Spirit, not fifty yards from the source spring which still bubbles out of the ground like a cauldron just north of the swimming pool dressing rooms.

The ledge was on private property, I guess, but I slipped through the barbed wire fence anyway and climbed the rocky slope. Sitting cross-legged atop the slab, which I had first seen over a hundred and fifty years ago, was like sitting in a time machine.

Leaves Always Green's deathbed was harder to pinpoint. The tree under which she rested was long gone. Everything along the river had been paved over and built up. The Ute camp had been so organic that it was all but invisible to me that first morning on the ledge. It had been replaced by masses of concrete and steel: fast-food eyesores, grasping steeples, gas pumps, "shiny animals," and endless pavement. I estimated the place of her death to be somewhere in the parking lot behind a business machines store.

Leaves Always Green had said that change, even the change we call death, is a natural part of life. Her words comforted me then. They comforted me now. Still, I found it jarring to see her resting place marked by a shop which filled its windows with four foot high signs screaming, "SALE! PC's AT ROCK BOTTOM PRICES."

Our front door closed with a solid *thunk*.

I studied Sandy from where I sat, compact as a cat, in the sunny window. Truth is, when the distance between us is enough to hide the tiny wrinkles that fan out from each eye toward her temples, she *does* look young enough to be my sister. Bouncy, open-faced, no makeup, hair in a pony tail. Pretty cute, I thought.

"One for me. One for you," Sandy announced. "Hmm. Looks like Jay's handwriting, but the return address is different."

"Thank you, Sandy. Would you like to read it first, or do you think it's safe for me to take it from here?" I said, snatching the envelope from her hand. Rather playfully I thought, but she hardly took notice. "Who's that from?"

"John," she said, and sat down at the table. "No stamp." She snapped the envelope with her finger, thinking. "He must have put it in our mailbox himself."

I opened the letter from Jay. It said he'd moved into a big house with four other guys. He had his own basement bedroom. They shared the kitchen and baths. It was noisy and two of his housemates were "pretty strange characters." But, all in all, he was happier there than with his uncle, who was drinking heavily every night. "He seems lost, really," Jay said. "Being successful, his big house and big bank account, hasn't made him happy. And I don't think things like that will make me happy either."

He said he was really getting into his anthropology course and might decide by next semester to declare it as his major. "Anthropologists apparently don't make lots of money," he said, "but it's work I think I'd really love."

He mentioned he'd be working over Thanksgiving weekend and wouldn't be home until the semester break at Christmas. I was disappointed, but not too surprised. It sounded like some kind of excuse, so he wouldn't have to choose between going through the motions of seeing me at Thanksgiving or having to tell me to get lost. Actually, I wouldn't have guessed a month ago that he would even still be writing by now. Why was he, anyway? Why string me along?

So his closing paragraph really caught me off guard:

> I'd like to see you at Christmas,
> and am hoping we can spend some
> time together. But I don't know
> what's going on with you. If you
> want to see me, even. I don't know
> how you feel about me.
>   — Jay

I was stunned. This was not a string along line. You don't go out of your way to ask to see someone you're trying to get rid of. But how could he think I might not care about seeing him? What had I said that could have upset him? Nothing, I assured myself. In fact, I'd taken considerable pains to censor my letters to Jay, making sure that no note of anger or hurt slipped in. *He* was the one who had left. *He* was the one with better places to go, better things to do. If he didn't care, I'd reasoned, why should I? My letters were civil and polite. I was sure I'd avoided anything that could hurt his feelings or reveal my own. So what was he complaining about?

I reread the last paragraph of his letter. I started again on my defense. But I didn't get very far before I stumbled onto the answer to my questions: Jay wasn't saying that I had hurt his feelings. He wasn't accusing me of anything. "I don't know what's going on with you. . . . I don't know how you feel about me." That's what he was saying.

And what had I said that might make him wonder if I cared about seeing him? Nothing. Which was exactly the problem. I hadn't written anything that meant anything. I'd kept him at a distance, hidden my feelings. I'd written of general happenings like some anonymous reporter. Nothing about myself. Nothing from inside.

Paper rattled as Sandy refolded the letter she'd been reading and slipped it into its envelope.

"Lisa, we need to talk," she said. My stomach tightened. She held up the envelope. "John's asking me to marry him again," she said simply.

150

"*Marry* him?" I said, wondering if she could hear the sudden thunder of my heart.

"Yes."

"Well, that's ridiculous. That's crazy." I laughed, but it was all nerves. Sandy didn't say anything. "You're not going to, are you? I mean, that's pretty insensitive of him. What do you mean 'again,' anyway?"

"He asked me, yesterday, if I would marry him," she said calmly. "I told him I couldn't answer him yet. That it was too soon. Now he's written me a letter —"

"A love letter," I accused. "That's what it is, isn't it?"

"I guess it is," she said shyly. "He says he loves me. That he wants to marry me. That we'd all be a family." Her voice was a little wavy. She cleared her throat. "But he understands it's too soon. He says he's willing to wait. As long as is necessary for me to make up my mind. It's very . . . really very nice," she finished.

"I can't believe it, Sandy! I can't believe you're even considering it!" I jumped up from the window seat and ran from the house.

Who does John Smith think he is? He's known my mother for all of what? A month and a half? My father's been dead for barely ten. It's too soon, all right. Way too soon, I kept thinking over and over as I ran to Genny's house. Happy family. *I* have something to say about that!

I wondered, will he be at the house when I get there? I don't care if he is. I won't let that stop me. I'm fifteen. Not some little kid. I'll tell him exactly what I think about his little plan.

151

From three doors up the street I saw that his car was gone.

Good, I thought. I hope he never comes back. I feel sorry for Genny. What kind of creep does she have for a father?

"My dad told me about asking your mom to marry him," Genny squealed when she met me at the door. She reached out to hug me. Something inside me snapped.

"*Your* dad. *Your* dad," I hissed, slapping her outstretched arms away. "Get it, Genny? He's *your* father, not mine. He'll never be my father. Not now. Not ever."

Genny didn't say anything. She just backed away as the force of my rage carried us to the middle of the living room. I was breathing hard and pouring all the hate I could into my voice and look. Genny didn't seem to be breathing at all. Her eyes focused somewhere past me. There were no tears, but her eyes were red and puffy, and a muscle near her mouth twitched. She dropped to the floor then, throwing her hands over her face and curling her lanky frame into a tight knot. She moaned and rocked, and I just stood there, looming over her like a giant, before I even realized she was crying.

"Genny," I said tentatively, crouching down and reaching out to touch her. She didn't respond. But still she cried, louder now. I sat there helpless on the rug beside her, remembering her joy at seeing me, and the hurt in her eyes when I slapped her away.

Seeing Genny like that, I hated myself. And I began to realize what I was doing to the people I loved most in the world. Blaming them for my hurt, pushing them away.

My mother when she tried to help. And Jay, when he left. Keeping him at a distance, protecting myself, just *because* he left. And now Genny, when all she wanted was to be my friend, my sister. A wave of compassion for her swept over me.

She lay sprawled by the couch, and I moved to sit against it. I rubbed her back lightly. "Genny," I said, but there was no response. "Genny," I tried again, "I'm so sorry. You didn't deserve that. It was me. It was just me."

She mumbled something, but from behind her hands it was unintelligible.

"What?" I asked, and gently tugged her hand away from her face.

"Don't," she said. "My nose is all runny."

I grabbed a box of tissues from the end table and passed it to her. She sat up against the couch, shoved long strands of red hair over her shoulder, and blew her nose.

"It's not just you," she said.

"What do you mean?"

"I mean, my mom didn't die in an avalanche."

"She didn't?"

Genny shook her head and blew her nose again. She heaved a big sigh.

"She left us." She looked at me as though she had just confessed a sin.

"Oh," was all I could think of to say.

"I made that story up, about the avalanche. Dad told me the truth from the start. But I didn't want anybody to know that she left me right after I was born. She left *him*, Dad always tells me. Big deal. I feel left anyway."

She draped a tissue over her face, mocking her own grief. But suddenly it possessed her again.

"And I *was* left," she wailed. "I was only a little baby. I was less than a month old!"

She grabbed another tissue, then threw the box across the room. It bounced off the faceless TV screen and the Beer Brothers were on it like mouse pie. She laughed a little, and I did, too, glad to get some feeling out.

"Anyway, this thing with your mom and my dad." She shrugged her shoulders apologetically. "It just sounded pretty good, I guess."

"Yeah," I said.

Genny slumped against me, her body as limp as a month-old carrot. I stroked her hair. My fingers, following their own mind, gently separated the tangles they found in the long, thick strands.

"It probably sounds stupid, but sometimes I still can't believe I never even really knew my own mother," she said.

"It doesn't," I said. "It's not stupid."

We sat there for a long time in silence, but inside my head everything was in an uproar. Genny's story had affected me strongly, in some way that I could feel but not fully understand. She had told me something important. And private. She had let me in, and I wanted to do the same with her. I didn't want to push people away anymore.

I tried to get hold of all the things I wanted to say. All the things I was feeling. All the things I was learning. If I could just do it, now, and in just the right way, Genny would be okay. I would, too. And I would know I was on a better path.

But it seemed like everything needed to be said at once. And no sooner did I get two thoughts in line than they would scatter like leaves in a breeze while I rounded up a third. It was nearly six o'clock, and overcast. The dark was coming on fast. Like the light, my chance was slipping away.

"I never told anyone about my mom before." Genny's words rolled off my shoulder into the dusk. They hung there, waiting for my reply. I searched for wise words. None came.

"Thanks, Genny." I rubbed my cheek against hers, and wished that I were a better human being. "I'm lucky to have a sister like you."

They were the only words I was able to find, and they didn't seem like much. So it surprised me, there in the dark, when I felt her smile.

17

The day broke golden and blue. As the sun topped the horizon I started up Mountain Avenue toward the hills. I wasn't sure what I wanted out of this journey. Things had been happening so fast. Maybe just some time by myself in a quiet place. The one I'd shared with Jay. Meditation Rock. I wanted to feel near him so I could write him the kind of letter he deserved. One about me, and my feelings.

Even though the air was sharp and crisp, by the time I got to the top of the hill two blocks from home I was sweating in my jacket. I stuffed it into my backpack with my lunch and paper and pen.

I turned off Mountain onto the road that Jay and I had taken, orange-flavored light at my back and my shadow leading the way. It was about five miles to the first turn-off. I should be there by 9:30, I calculated. Even allowing for a couple of short rest breaks I should be to the rock an hour after that. Plenty of time to write, eat, rest up, and still get back home by six. Before sunset.

I remembered all the friendly people I'd waved to that summer day with Jay. Now it was early October, and early in the day, too. Even so, the sun was already hot on my back; the light, cool breeze, welcome and refreshing. My feet felt good in the hiking boots Genny helped me pick out. I felt like I could walk forever.

But by the time the road turned to gravel I wasn't so sure. My legs were tired and my shoulders complained bitterly about the pack that bounced and tugged with every step. And I was starving. Time for a break. I checked my watch: 9:27, and still nearly two miles to the turn-off. I was a slower hiker than I thought.

Five minutes later I was on the move again, my engine stoked with apple energy and a few handfuls of trail mix. When I did reach the turn-off I was forty minutes behind schedule. It was farther than I expected to the national forest path, too, but when I got there it was like stepping through an invisible doorway into another world. A thin carpet of leaves cushioned me underfoot. Gnarly white-trunked aspen, their leaves turned gold and pink and copper since my last visit, chattered noisily to me as I passed by. I found where we had parked the car, crossed the meadow quickly and soon was crunching over cinnamon-stained pine needles which littered the floor of the ponderosa forest.

Like everything else, the pond seemed farther than I remembered. But finally the water, shrunken to a puddle now, lay before me and I was surrounded on three sides by the huge granite rocks Jay and I had climbed.

A sound in the brush nearby startled me. Suddenly I felt like an alien, trespassing and vulnerable, in a place I didn't belong. And although I caught a reassuring glimpse of a tiny creature skittering under a fallen pine, every new sound made me think a bear or mountain lion was about to pounce on me from the curtain of trees. I clambered up the rocks as fast as I could, scratching my hands and banging my knees all the way. On top, with a far horizon and free from hidden attack, I felt safe again.

The view from Meditation Rock was incredible. Large stands of golden aspen punctuated the landscape. I flashed back to the experience of beauty and belonging that I had here before, and waved to the magnificent hillside and the snow-covered peaks beyond. "You're beautiful," I said and, emboldened by the sound of my own voice, called out louder. "You're beautiful!" The echo bounced back to me and I smiled.

I was not an alien here. I was merely alone in the wilderness for the first time in my life. And that was all right. More than all right. It was perfect.

I unpacked the remains of my lunch — a banana, another apple, and a few ounces of trail mix — and checked my watch: 11:50. Four hours since I'd left home, instead of the two and a half I'd planned on. I decided I should head back no later than two o'clock. Not as much time as I'd figured to have, but enough.

The food was gone in a hurry. Oh well, easier to carry it inside than on my back. I pulled out my writing paper. Not much wind this time. That would make writing easier. But it was cooler up here than down below. I slipped my jacket back on.

It turned out to be a long letter. I told Jay how important he was to me. How much I looked forward to being with him at Christmas. I poured out all the feelings I'd been holding in — about him, Genny, my joy at being at Meditation Rock this day. I thanked him for telling me about his grandmother and told him about my new friend,

Mrs. MacGregor. How we both missed him. About all the work we had done cleaning the garden and preparing the soil for spring planting, which I wouldn't miss for anything. About the ears of corn we'd saved, "for Halloween," Mrs. MacGregor had said, "and for seed in the spring."

When I finished writing, the sun had hardly moved in the sky, but it had weakened somehow. And the wind had sharpened.

I folded the six pages neatly and slipped them into the zippered side pocket of my pack. I felt good about it. And ready for lunch again, too. I satisfied myself as best I could by scrounging a few crumbs from the trail mix sack and taking another swig of water. I checked my watch. Half an hour left. I decided to spend it at Singing Waters.

The path to the water was strewn with aspen leaves. I felt like I was walking on hundreds of gold coins dropped carelessly from a pirate's treasure chest. Beauty surrounded me. I was rich. I'd thought I would miss Missouri's fall colors, but there were reds and oranges here, too. And pink and purple. And a dozen shades of green. They were just more subtly displayed, hidden away in miniature bushes and in lichens smothering the granite boulders. All highlighted by the glorious golds and yellows of the aspen and the willows. And above them, through the lattice-work of branches, the ever-blue Colorado sky.

Except it wasn't quite so blue just now, I noticed. A thin veil of transparent clouds covered half the sky and softened the sun's rays. I zipped my jacket.

I always thought being alone in the mountains would be unnervingly quiet. I was wrong. Earlier I had been unnerved by nature's noises. Now, water flowing over the stones tinkled like chimes in the wind. A jaybird with a black crest shrieked at me as he hopped nervously from branch to branch in a nearby willow. Maybe I was too near for his comfort or maybe he'd never even seen a human being before. Little feet scurried in the underbrush and I watched a pair of chipmunks — watching me — take turns darting in and out of crevices in a nearby rock. Flies buzzed as though they were sharing a midsummer picnic, and a *clickety-click*ing rattlesnake behind me turned out to be a grasshopper. From time to time there was the twitter of aspen leaves in the gusting breeze, and always, the modulated moan of faraway wind as it rushed through hills and trees.

A mass of grey clouds swelled in the northwest. Shivering, I pulled my jacket zipper tight to the neck and decided it was time to start back. As I climbed the steep path I found some wild rose bushes, their tiny leaves turned scarlet, the swollen red fruits nodding from their stems, just as Jay had predicted. With more than a seven-mile hike ahead of me and hungry already, I decided it was time to taste-test the rosehips.

The skin was tart; the pulp around the seeds was sweet. Not so bad. I tried another, then two at once, which made it a bit difficult to sort the seeds out successfully. Definitely edible, even kind of tasty, but it would take some time to fill an empty stomach on these. Time that I didn't have just now. I picked a small handful and dumped them in my jacket pocket to show Mrs. MacGregor.

The clouds overhead had thickened, blocking the disk of the sun and sliding like a navy-blue sheet toward the east. The dark backdrop accentuated the golden brightness of the aspen which seemed to glow with fluorescent leaves in the sudden gloom. A drop of rain spattered my cheek. As I looked up two more fat ones slapped my face. I pulled my jacket hood over my head and, in what fast became a downpour, stumbled up the slickening path, searching for shelter, hoping I wouldn't need it for long.

Near the top of the trail that led back to the meadow I came upon several car-sized boulders, tumbled against each other so as to form a small cave underneath. It was getting cold. The rain was changing to snow by the time I crawled inside.

I crouched down, wrapped my arms around myself, and huddled there on the dry dirt like a rabbit, protected for the moment from the large, wet flakes which were falling thick and fast. Protected but not safe. Not from the cold, which already penetrated my wet clothing. And not from the fear, which was rising from my gut in a tidal wave of panic.

The sky darkened further and the wind intensified, carrying the snow almost horizontally. Before my eyes, the world whitened. Aspen leaves, abandoning their safe perches, launched themselves into brief and reckless flight before skidding to their final resting places, dappling the earth's new blanket with gold.

By 3:30 I was shivering and could not stop, and the leaden sky still poured thick, heavy snow with no sign of letting up. Like someone trapped in a slowly sinking ship I watched the snow level rise in front of me. Finally, all the leaves and grass were buried. Reality hit like the shock wave from a bomb blast: I am mortal. And death might not come when I'm old and waiting for it. It might come today.

Self-pity welled up. I would die alone, here in the cold and the white. In this very spot. My body, scavenged and scattered by animals, would never even be found. My letter would never get to Jay. He would never know how much I cared for him. I wouldn't get to be Genny's sister anymore. Mrs. MacGregor. Who would help her with spring planting? And my mother. All the time and energy we'd wasted on blame and petty squabbling. Now my only wish was that I had loved her better.

And still the snow came. Everything was white. Beautiful but deadly. White.

. . . *white walls slip by as I race down the hall. I'd heard a groan. A startled yelp, cut short. Something heavy falling in the study . . . My father, still as death on the floor, barely breathing; his right arm clutching his chest as though he would massage his own heart back to health . . .*

My finger shakes out of control. I stab the wrong number, curse, and dial again. What's our address, the emergency dispatcher wants to know? Precious seconds slip by before I can say it right. The too-calm voice guides me through . . .

162

I talk to my father, but he doesn't answer. He doesn't move. I don't know if he can hear me . . . The voice on the phone tells me to tilt his head back, breathe into his mouth, pump his chest. I do it . . . four unearthly minutes pass . . .

Thunder on the steps. Unfamiliar voices in the hall. Garbled words surround me . . . Orange-suited arms lift me to my feet, shepherd me to a corner. Out of the way . . . A plastic mask is over my father's nose and mouth, a needle pushes into his arm. People I don't know buckle him roughly onto a stretcher, like baggage . . .

The next morning, the phone rings . . .

I hate you, I screamed inside. For not giving me time to prepare. I hate you! Not even a goodbye. I hate you! I hate you!

"I hate you," I whispered. "I hate you!" I said again, shocked to hear the awful words reverberating in my ears, profaning my sanctuary and the memory of my father. But once unleashed, my tongue would not stop. "I hate you for not knowing about your heart problem. For not telling me about it. For not taking care of yourself. I hate you for dying. I hate you for leaving."

It was horrifying at first, but the feeling of release was so rewarding that it was easy to keep on. "I hate you, for leaving Sandy and me alone, for loving me and then going away without any warning." My voice was stronger, more certain. "For not being here, now, when I need you. I hate you for letting me love you. It wasn't fair. It wasn't fair!" I cried out. "I don't care who hears me. I hate you for dying!"

163

I was panting. Hot tears ran down my face and made dark circles on my snow-dusted pants. "Oh, Daddy," I said softly, "I miss you."

... Leaves Always Green gazes up at me from where she lies beneath the massive ponderosa pine. "Do not hold others with your grief, or death becomes a horror. ... Do not hold others with your grief ..."

I visualized my father going to the Spirit Light that Leaves Always Green spoke of. I hoped it was a good place.

"Goodby, Dad," I whispered. "I still love you."

Images of Catherine MacGregor and Einstein and even the table that Mrs. MacGregor's husband had made rushed through my mind. I hoped it was okay, letting go.

"Goodbye," I said again.

I was exhausted. Cold again, too, and weaker than before. And without food, dry clothing, or matches. I looked out at six inches of snow. My watch said 4:45. If I didn't want to spend the night here, the rest of my life maybe, it was time to do something.

With cold-numbed fingers I felt for the rosehips in my pocket, found them, and pulled them out. Thirteen. My lucky number, I decided. I set the four puniest ones aside, then devoured the other nine, spitting the seeds emphatically to one side of my shelter. It was not a meal. It was a ceremony. These nine tiny fruits will sustain me for as long as need be, I vowed. I slipped the remaining four back into my pocket. They would be distributed later — to Jay, Genny, Mrs. MacGregor, and Sandy — when I told each of them my story.

I left my shelter and trudged uphill. I knew only the general direction and that I had to keep going up to get to the meadow. The path was totally obliterated. The storm had transformed the landscape, and still the snow came. It fell straight down now, surrounding me like an impenetrable curtain. My hands and face were bitter cold. Snow was sneaking in over the tops of my boots and I knew my feet would soon be colder yet. The crunch of snow and my own breathing were the only sounds I heard. No birds, no chipmunks, no Singing Waters.

Something moved, fast and low, at the edge of my vision. I heard a growl. I stopped instantly and shrunk down as if that would somehow protect me. Then came a deep, throaty bark. Coyotes, I wondered? Wolves?

A large, white, shaggy-haired animal materialized from the background of snow. It growled, low and menacing, and watched me every second. I stayed crouched, afraid to move. Again it barked. I hoped it was a dog. But even if it was, it was a *big* dog.

Now other noises came. I caught glimpses of moving patches of brown, dirty white, black. There were a lot of them. And they all appeared to be as big or bigger than the first, who still had me pinned to this defenseless spot. I'd heard about domesticated dogs, abandoned or runaways, that join in packs, roaming the mountains, growing wilder every day. Should I scream? Run? Hold my ground? I looked around, searching for a weapon.

The forms crept toward me out of the woods. Four, five, six, nine, ten, twelve. As the pack closed on me I began to see that these were not dogs. They were something else. And a swinging udder told me what. Goats! Brown goats, black goats, brown and white goats. My furry jailer was the only dog. He was big and full of threat, but he had not moved a step toward me and, surrounded now by the goats, he seemed less vicious. The goats stayed in a close group, moving like a blob of protoplasm, and disappeared again into the curtain of snow. Their protector watched me until the last of his charges was safely out of my sight, then bounded off after them.

I was relieved at first, but not for long. I had just let slip away the only living, breathing beings I was likely to find out here. They must have come from somewhere and they just might know exactly where that somewhere was. A warm house, hopefully, with a telephone and a hot shower. I prayed it wasn't far, but anything was better than stumbling blindly through the woods. It was 5:20, and although the unseen sun was still somewhere above the horizon, the light was failing fast.

Pointing myself in the direction of their retreat I ran through the snow on numbed feet, stumbling over hidden rocks and brush. After what seemed like forever without seeing or hearing them I came upon the animals' tracks. I trailed the herd, keeping just far enough back not to provoke an attack from the dog, but close enough to keep him in sight and hearing.

In the near dark, just before six, I detected a familiar smell in the air. Smoke! I rushed forward, then stopped short as the trees gave way to a sudden clearing.

166

Had I slipped back in time again somehow? A log cabin stood short and squat under sagging, snow-laden pines. Soft light glowed from the windows and yellowed little squares of snow outside. Smoke curled out of a chimney. The goats and dog wandered over to a barn, the dog barking almost casually at me now over his shoulder. I was convinced the scene was nineteenth-century until I noticed the pickup and four-wheel drive.

A man and a woman came out of the house. They shouted "Hello." I shouted back. The man went to the goats.

"Come on in," the woman said. "You look cold."

Underdressed and hungry and lost and not as smart as a goat, too, but if she thought it she was kind enough not to say it.

The cabin was just one room, about the size of our livingroom. Besides a wood-fired cookstove that dominated one wall, there was a work table, a table and chairs for dining, an odd looking refrigerator, something that I imagined must be a spinning wheel, and a bed. The place was snug and warm, like being under the blankets in a hugely oversized bed. The stove poured out heat along with the wonderful smell of baking bread.

"My name's Landis. What's yours?" She pushed me toward a chair and grabbed off my soaked jacket. Wavy, russet hair framed her cat-like face.

"Lisa," I answered, "Lisa Carey. I'm from Indian Springs. Could I use your phone?"

"You could if we had one," she smiled. She sliced through a large loaf of bread that was cooling near the stove. "Better move that chair over here," she said. "You'll dry off faster." I did as I was told and she placed a cup of steaming coffee and a thick slice of buttered bread before me. I was so hungry I ate it all and drank the hot black coffee without even looking up.

When I was finished, Landis whisked the plate away and asked, "What are you doing out in this storm? Did you walk all the way from Indian Springs?"

I nodded. "It seemed so warm this morning. It was lucky I saw your dog and the goats. I was getting cold. And a little lost, too," I admitted.

"Well, you *were* lucky to cross paths with our little tribe, but you were plain smart to follow them," she said, skillfully finding the bright spot in what others might see as a rather dismal tale.

"What kind of dog is he, anyway?" I asked. "I've never seen one like him."

"He's a she. Her name is Frost. She's part Komondor and part Great Pyrenees. Makes a good guard dog for the herd. It would take a pretty brave and pretty stupid coyote to attack with her around." She took three more brown loaves from the cavernous oven. "Bob'll be back in a minute from tending the animals. He'll drive you home. You want another slice?"

"Thanks. That would be wonderful," I said. "The ride, too, if it's not any trouble."

"Oh, it's a little trouble," she said, putting another chunk of bread in front of me. "But it's not nearly so much for him to drive you as it would be for you to walk." She smiled.

"I guess not," I said. "Thanks." I finished off the second helping nearly as quickly as the first. "Can I use your bathroom, please?" I said.

"No bathroom, either. Got an outhouse, though. Just out back."

"Oh." I wasn't used to outhouses. And it was cold out there. "I can wait." The heat from the stove was soothing. "I'm really glad you're here," I murmured. Listlessness was seeping into every muscle.

"Us, too," Landis said. "We don't have much in the way of utilities but we've got lots of beauty and freedom. Bob and I looked all over the country and half the rest of the world before we settled down here. Our friends and family thought it was a bad idea. Warned us against it. 'You can't live without electricity, neighbors, etc., etc.,' they said. But you know, you find something that feels right, you want your friends and family to encourage and support you to take the risk, make the change. This felt right. A good place to grow old in. So, we did it anyway."

She smiled her big smile again. I thought of my mother. She'd made some changes, too. And she loved being in Indian Springs. I hadn't been much help to her.

Cold air and snow blew in with Bob. "Goats are settled down for a cold winter's night . . . in October," he said, his big red face breaking out in a sudden laugh.

"Gotta get this girl home, Bob, before we get rounded up for kidnapping," Landis joked. She plopped a black and white woven hat on my head and pulled it snugly over my ears. "Trixie would want you to have this," she said.

"Your daughter?" I asked, wondering where she could be hidden.

"Not exactly. Trixie's one of the goats," Landis explained. "Angora. I made this myself. I'd like you to have it, too."

"Thanks," I said.

The four-wheel drive truck chugged along the invisible drive away from Landis' and Bob's homestead. A yellow light shone out the window. All around was soft white snow. I caught a glimpse of Frost, a hump of white against the dark barn siding — a sentinel at her post.

Come back and visit, Landis had said.

I will, I'd promised.

And I would bring my mother. She would like these people as much as I did.

18

"Something from Jay," Sandy said, bursting into my room. She was fingering a long yellow envelope. "Feels like little rocks inside."

Sandy hadn't accepted John Smith's proposal of marriage yet, but I was sure it was only a matter of time. And, although we hadn't really discussed it since the arrival of his letter, my sense was that Sandy's slow response was more for my sake than hers. He was willing to wait for her and she was willing to wait for me.

And I was getting used to the idea. I'd had a lot of time lately to think. For four days I'd been sick in bed with a bad cold. I never saw Sandy so angry as the day Bob drove me home. She yelled and sent me to my room and I was too flabbergasted, too exhausted, and too embarrassed to do anything but go. That night she sat on the edge of my bed, telling me how worried she'd been, how she'd called the sheriff's department to report me missing, and that John and Genny had driven the county roads looking for me.

I felt bad about all the trouble I'd caused, apologized as best I could to Sandy, then called Genny and her dad to do the same.

The next morning I had a fever and sore throat, both much worse by midday. Genny tried to visit, but Sandy wouldn't let her for fear of contagion. She looked in on me every hour, brought me juices, and generally treated me like a sick little kid. And, sick little kid that I was, I appreciated it.

The following day, Monday, I was worse and Sandy stayed home from work. But then the fever broke and almost immediately I felt immensely better, although it was impossible to convince Sandy. She stayed home the rest of the day, getting her money's worth out of the fever thermometer. Perhaps because the crisis had passed she went back to giving mini-lectures on the irresponsibility of my behavior and the pain it had caused. I didn't argue.

My friends were a big help. Genny dropped by on Tuesday after school and Michael and Chris, too, a little later. They had no respect for the recently near-dead and they made me laugh so hard I felt almost healthy for hours. Mrs. MacGregor heard the news somehow and sent over a bag of herbs which Sandy steeped for tea.

And now Genny was here again, telling me gossipy tales from school and, in between, reading my biology assignment to me. Of course, she was more interested in my mail.

"Could be diamonds!" Genny suggested with perfect seriousness. "Let me see, let me see," she begged, reaching for the envelope. But Sandy placed it into my hand, and with a cheery "Bye girls," left us alone.

"Do you think he got your letter and is answering it already or did they cross in the mail?" Genny asked.

"I don't know, Genny."

And I was afraid to guess. Either way it seemed ominous. The postmark was from Boulder, Tuesday morning. I'd mailed my letter Saturday evening, on my way home with Bob, in order to get it in before the last dispatch. Jay probably received it on Monday. It was possible, probable even, that he'd gotten my letter, written back and mailed it immediately. But was that good or bad? And what had he sent?

I explored the envelope, squeezing the contents between my fingers. Rough, hard, all pretty much the same size. Probably a traditional Ute brush-off, sending pebbles to the one you hate.

"Well, open it already," Genny urged, apparently fearful that I might not. I slipped my nail under the loose pucker at one end and slid it quickly along the length of the packet, cutting my finger on the paper's edge. I sucked the blood while Genny, too impatient for first-aid at a time like this, dumped the envelope on its side. A tiny rockslide cascaded onto the bed. But they were not rocks. They were . . . corn. Several dozen pieces of dried corn.

I reached inside the envelope and pulled out Jay's very short note:

> Got your wonderful letter. Don't
> you and Mrs. MacGregor plant these
> next spring without me. See you at
> Christmas.
>
> — Jay

"Corn? What does that mean?" Genny wanted to know.

Two powerful images sprang into my mind: Jay and I and Mrs. MacGregor in her beautiful garden, and he and I hiking in the mountains, surrounded by wildflowers.

"It means . . . everything," I said, smiling.

"Great!" she answered, as if the news were her own good fortune.

Finally, mid-November, I felt back to normal. And it was then that I had the dream.

. . . Spirit calls for help. Her voice is small but she isn't a little girl. She isn't calling "Papa." She is calling me. She looks a little older now than I have ever seen her as she lies there in the grass near the river by the hot springs. Lush green grass all around her, willow leaves unfolding, the sun warm and high. But even in this brightness of midday a falling star shoots across the sky above her . . .

I woke with a jolt and looked at the clock: 1:02, NOV. 17, the steady orange glow declared. The date seemed significant, familiar, but I couldn't think why. My only clear thought — almost an instinct — was that I had to get to the pool and to Spirit. It was more than two months since I last saw her. Not since Leaves Always Green died.

I worried about sneaking out of the house, especially after my near-disastrous adventure. But the sense of urgency was so compelling that it drove me from the bed. If explanations were necessary, I decided, I would just have to give them. Later.

On my way to the pool I noticed five shooting stars. November 17! That was the date Mr. Burrows said would probably be the peak of the Leonid shower this year. Fear nagged at me. The same scared feeling I remembered having at the close of Mr. Burrows's class that day I sat in.

Cold air thickened the steam from the pool and I could barely see Spirit through it. I hadn't even called her name this time. She was just there, as if she'd been waiting for me. I jumped in. Our hands touched.

There was the Ute camp, settled peacefully in the meadow, as usual. But where was Spirit? Why had she called me?

. . . Leaves Always Green and Spirit, sitting at the edge of the pool. "I knew that the stars were falling to bring you to us," Leaves Always Green says. "You would dream with us for a time. Then go as you came . . ."

A riderless red-brown horse shot past me, glistening with sweat. Her huge eyes bulged and she snorted with excitement. Circling sharply in the meadow, she accelerated again, this time toward the spot where I stood. She stopped a dozen feet away, pawing the ground and exhaling noisily. Then she walked right up to me. She turned broadside. Three parallel ragged streaks, as long as my open hand, glistened red in the quivering muscle of her left flank. She stood motionless. Waiting.

Although I had never before in my life so much as touched a horse, something inside told me to reach up and grab the mane — and in one magical moment I was atop the animal's back! Immediately she turned and headed back from where she had come, quickly gaining speed as she shifted through a series of flesh and blood gears. I lay down against her back and neck, holding on for dear life.

She zigzagged through trees, then burst out of the obstacle course and galloped toward the river. I saw a large bear, his wet fur streaming water, wade out onto the far bank. My horse stopped and turned, so suddenly that I was nearly flung to the ground. Then Colorow was hurrying towards us on his big brown and white stallion. He paid me no attention as he brought the animal up sharply, jumped to the ground and ran toward the river through knee-high grass.

That was when I saw her. Spirit was lying almost invisible in the tall grass, not far from the bank. I slipped off my mount and ran to where she lay, both dreading and knowing what I would find. She was so still. Her eyes were closed, her face white, her neck angled strangely to the side.

When Colorow reached her, a moment after me, she opened her eyes. He stroked her forehead softly. Her eyes closed. I felt the life force in her fading fast.

Why am I here? Why am I here? I asked the universe. It was Leaves Always Green who answered.

". . . The snowflake falls to the ground, melts in its season, and greens the earth. We complete our circle and go to the Spirit Light . . ."

"Spirit," I said, leaning in close to her ear. Could she hear me? I didn't even know if she was still alive. "Spirit, it's Lisa. Remember what Leave Always Green said. When your cycle on earth is over, don't cling to the earth.

176

Just let go. Go to the Spirit Light. Do you see it? Look for it, Spirit. And when you find it, don't be afraid. Don't hang on. Just go to the light."

I was splitting apart. Part of me floated up over the springs. Light, pure light, all around. I wasn't me anymore. Not like before. I was light. Spirit was light. Just warmth and light, everywhere.

I could no longer see Spirit, but I could feel her presence. I knew that our separation was imminent. I knew, too, that it was only an illusion. We would always be together. No longer at the pool, or in her village. But somewhere, in the light.

Spirit's hand grazed mine like a breath of wind. A moment later I stood on the balcony. The hot springs pool was peaceful.

I knew I needn't come again.

19

The next day it was seventy-three degrees, matching the record for November, set in nineteen-fifty-something. About six inches of dirty snow, left from a series of small storms that had started on the day of my hike, transformed itself into a torrent of water in the city streets and muddy footprints from one end of school to the other. By evening it was gone altogether and the yard grass looked like a reedy, woven mat. Sandy and I sat in the porch swing, talking and watching the night sky.

"There goes one," I said, pointing to a slow-moving shooting star with a long, filmy trail.

"And there," she said, almost the next moment, as a brilliant flash pierced the sky for an instant.

"This is still part of the Leonid shower. Mr. Burrows says it's from a comet."

"Messengers from the gods, my grandmother called them," Sandy said.

"I like that," I said, thinking of Spirit and Leaves Always Green. They were something like shooting stars themselves: free and beautiful, brightening my thoughts. My guides. My messengers.

"You know, Lisa, I had to make this move. It wasn't just the job. There were too many reminders in our old home. Here's where he sat at meals, this was his favorite

178

chair when he watched TV. The whole city, even. Where we got married, walked in the park together, had our first kiss." Her hands flashed from side to side, mapping her memories of Dad on our front porch. "And his study. All those books."

I touched her shoulder. "Sandy —" I said.

She shook her head. "No. I want to say this. I need to." She swallowed. A moment passed. "The books were hard. The books were *him*." She looked at me quickly, a thin beseeching smile on her face.

"I know," I said. "It's okay."

"Your dad and I didn't have a lot of interests in common, but we loved each other, from first to last. And we always supported each other. I wanted a baby right away. Your dad wanted to wait. He was still in graduate school. We argued. We debated. We cried. But once we made the decision and I got pregnant, he was with me all the way. And he loved you so much. He told me it was the best argument he ever lost."

She smiled.

"And you. You were so like him. Still are," she continued. "I admit I was a little jealous of all the things you did together. Sometimes I wished you and I shared more interests, so we could spend more time with each other. And now you're almost grown up and I'll lose you altogether. You'll go away . . ."

"Go away? Where am I going?" I had no idea.

"It won't be long you'll be heading off to college."

College. How I had longed for it. Ever since I was old enough to know where it was that Dad went every day, that it was books and knowledge and ideas that made him who he was, I had wanted to go to college. And, since coming to Indian Springs, college had taken on another meaning: escape. But escape wasn't on my mind anymore. Besides, college was a million years away, in a dim, intangible future. But here was Mom, talking about it as if I were leaving tomorrow.

"But Mom." She looked at me quickly, as though I had startled her somehow. "I'm only fifteen."

A fragile smile escaped from somewhere inside her. "'Only fifteen,' she says. 'Only fifteen.' Don't forget: I knew you when you were zero."

"Okay, so you knew me when I was zero, and now I'm an old lady of fifteen who just might go off to college, assuming tenth grade will end some day. I mean, people have been known to return from college. There are rumors about it all the time. It's in the papers." She smiled bigger.

Especially when they have reasons to return, I thought. Good feelings, and good friends. Like Genny. And Jay. Landis and Bob. Mrs. MacGregor, who I knew would be here forever, one way or another. Along with Colorow, and Leaves Always Green, and Spirit. And even Dad, whom I'd laid to rest, finally, in these mountains.

Maybe Landis was right. This just might be a good place to grow old in. Time would tell. I didn't think we were losing each other, Mom and I. Just the opposite.

"Oh! Look at that one!" she said, slapping my knee as she leaned forward, pointing at the sky.

I leaned and looked, too: the shimmering trail of a falling star, fading like a dream.

Further Reading

Berger, Melvin. *Comets, Meteors and Asteroids*. New York: G. P. Putnam's Sons, 1981.

Brown, Dee. *Bury My Heart At Wounded Knee: An Indian History of the American West*. New York: Bantam, 1970.

Cahill, Rick. *Colorado Hot Springs Guide*. Boulder: Pruett Publishing Company, 1983.

Croswell, Ken. "Will The Lion Roar Again?" *Astronomy*, November 1991.

Emmitt, Robert. *The Last War Trail: The Utes And The Settlement Of Colorado*. Norman: University of Oklahoma Press, 1954.

Givón, T. (ed.). *Ute Traditional Narratives*. Ignacio, Colorado: Ute Press, 1985.

Jefferson, James; Delaney, Robert W.; and Thompson, Gregory C. *The Southern Utes: A Tribal History*. Ignacio, Colorado: Southern Ute Tribe, 1972.

Marsh, Charles S. *People Of The Shining Mountains*. Boulder, Colorado: Pruett Publishing, 1982.

Pettit, Jan. *Utes: The Mountain People*. Boulder, Colorado: Johnson Books, 1990.

Smith, Anne M. *Ethnography Of The Northern Utes*. Santa Fe: Museum Of New Mexico Press, 1974.

Urquhart, Lena M. *Colorow: The Angry Chieftain*. Denver: The Golden Bell Press, 1968.

ABOUT THE AUTHORS

Terry and Wayne Baltz were born and raised in St. Louis, although at the time they were better known as Terry Swekosky and Wayne Baltz. They now live in Colorado, where they divide their time between living in the city (with the luxury of indoor plumbing) and living in their one-room cabin in the mountains (with the luxuries of far views, deer and elk, badgers, mountain bluebirds, coyotes, eagles, and incredibly starry nights).

The authors regularly visit schools, where they talk with children about writing, book publishing, and the creative process. You may contact them at 970/493-6593, or at the publisher's address, for further information.